The Fifth Branch

Kate Samuels

Harkraven Press

THE FIFTH BRANCH

First edition. August 1, 2021.

Copyright © 2021 Kate Samuels.

ISBN: 978-1777542528

Written by Kate Samuels.

To Mom, for Wales

Table of Contents

Foreword

Most Americans can't find Wales on a map. I credit Lloyd Alexander's *Chronicles of Prydain,* which sat on my bookshelf all through my childhood, for prompting me to forsake the University of British Columbia for a sophomore semester in Cardiff. Alexander was an American soldier who fell in love with Wales during World War II. His fictional Prydain was, in his own words, "not to be used as a guide for tourists," but it worked well enough for me—over the course of the semester, Celtic hill forts, Roman foundations, Norman mottes, Marcher fortresses, a Saxon dyke, and a jumble of retold mythological and historical anecdotes gleaned from books, plaques, tourist brochures, Dr. Juliette Wood, Wikipedia, and random locals who adopted me for the day found their way onto my travel blog, *Wales Watching.* I was particularly taken with the Four Branches of the Mabinogi, four interconnected myths short on internal logic but long on whimsy. They were set to paper probably in the twelfth century, but they're seeded (if you're inclined toward a certain romanticism) with tantalizing traces of an older, lost oral tradition.

The outline of this novel came together in the back row of a Welsh culture and mythology course taught by the inimitable Dr. Juliette Wood, internationally renowned Merlin expert and owner of the plummiest British accent I've ever been blessed to hear. I hope she will pardon me for playing it fast and loose with the mythology: any liberties, mistakes, or glaring Americanisms are decidedly mine.

Chapter 1: Reading Magic

I've learned not to trust the eggs in the fridge. To start with, it's a student fridge, which means the salami on the bottom shelf expired in the Paleolithic. I won't start on the smell, which is a subtle potpourri of every meal we never got around to cooking, laced with subtle notes of that one onion I bought back in October. But the eggs are something special.

I'll come back to the eggs.

The place to begin is last July, when Cardiff Uni sent out the roommate survey. It asked the usual stuff. Drinking? As long as you share. Early riser? Not on your life. Magic? My Dungeons and Dragons character is a half-orc druid; I wouldn't mind seeing a bit of magic up close. The magic majors at my home uni are cliquey. I don't think they'd want to share with a non-maj even if the non-maj was game.

So...I checked the box. And got Aurelia Ambrose.

Aurelia of the horoscopes and crystals. Aurelia of the levitating calculator. Aurelia of the two kettles ("for disgusting potions," "not for disgusting potions"). Aurelia, who knocks on your door at four a.m. with an empty jam jar. She doesn't want you to *kill* the giant harvester spider in the bathroom. No, she wants you to chase the sucker around the flat for half an hour, and she's mad when you accidentally knock off one of its legs. And when you finally stuff the awful thing into the jar, she won't let you dump it out the window, because it might sit there on the wall waiting to drop on her head when she leaves the building for class. No, she wants you to walk it all the way across the street and toss it in the neighbor's bushes. Then she accidentally locks you out.

I may have mentioned a levitating calculator. It was mine, and it was fifteen minutes before my Archaeological Methods lab.

Most roommates give you food poisoning. Aurelia gives you *poison* poisoning. We're now a three-kettle household. I keep mine in my room.

But...the eggs.

It was a rainy Tuesday in February. I'd been in Cardiff for six months. By that time, I spoke about as much Welsh as most Cardiffians, which is to say, I was fluent in street sign. I knew the cheapest places for cream tea and curry pasties. I could read a rail map. I could convert Canadian dollars to British pounds in my head. I'd been to every interesting archaeological site and museum within an hour of Cardiff. I'd adopted "bloody" as a catch-all sentence enhancer. I was familiar enough with Wetherspoons to start calling it Spoons. I'd lost interest in my travel blog, which meant I'd stopped feeling like a traveler and started feeling like a temporary local.

Aurelia had Conceptual Pescothaumaturgy that morning, so I had the flat to myself. I put on my headphones and set out to make a hearty English breakfast, or as close as I could manage in a kitchenette whose cooking arsenal consisted of an electric burner, a nonstick wok pan, and a fork. I toasted bread and cherry tomatoes in the wok and dumped them on a plate, set tea steeping, and poured the rest of the boiling water into the wok. I picked myself the biggest egg from the carton. They were Aurelia's eggs, so I wasn't surprised they were all different shapes and sizes. She was a farmer's market girl. I wasn't even sure all the eggs came from chickens. This one was brown and veiny and big enough to fill my palm. Maybe I should've paid more attention. But I hadn't had my caffeine yet.

I was going for soft-boiled. I dropped it in the wok and turned away to wrestle the canned beans open with the handle of the fork. And since I had Ed Sheeran turned up loud, I didn't hear the splashing. I didn't notice anything till I backed up and put my foot in a hot puddle.

I spun. Boiling water was slopping over the rim of the wok. Panic ensued. I couldn't turn off the stove, because there was boiling water running over the dial, and every time water hit the burner, it went up in steam, which fogged up my glasses. So I went on thinking the wok had just boiled over, right up till the moment a wing flopped over the rim.

The wing was disproportionately small, almost vestigial, and sort of batlike, but red. It was thin, and it stuck to the pan like wet fabric. I heard sizzling.

Adrenaline's a funny thing. I pitched my tea and used the mug to scoop the tiny dragon out of the water.

When I tried to dump him and his boiling bath in the sink, his wings stuck to the side of the mug. Then one of them flopped free and stuck to me. Then he bit my thumb. It hurt. He finally fell out of the mug and smacked onto the sink rack, all tangled up in my tea bag.

I set down the mug very carefully. I'd scalded my fingers. They stung. I wanted to wash my hands with cold water and soap, but I also didn't want to put my hands back in nipping range.

The steam cleared. There was a small red dragon in my sink.

He wasn't quite as red as the dragon on the Welsh flag. He had beady little eyes under ridged brows. His tail was thrice the length of the rest of him and ended in an arrowhead. He must've been packed pretty tight in that egg, because now that he'd unfolded, he was about the size of my brother's pet rat.

I watched him for a minute to make sure he wasn't going to climb out of the sink. On further consideration, I got the colander and put it over him. Then I went for my phone.

"Aurelia?" I said.

Students in the UK don't major in a subject; they "read" it. I've always thought that's a feeble verb for what goes on in a magic lab. Judging by the sounds in the background when you call a magic major in class, they don't *read* Conceptual Pescothaumaturgy. They squelch it. Possibly battle it with forceps. Occasionally slap it into submission. "Hi, Marlene!" Aurelia said brightly. "I'll call back in fifteen minutes."

"Don't!" I didn't mean to bark at her, but the adrenaline was still going strong.

"Oh. Okay."

"I need you to tell me what I just hatched and what I'm supposed to do about it."

"Huh?"

"The eggs," I said. "I wanted a soft-boiled egg and I got a pet."

"Oh. Crap. You hatched my term project."

"What was your term project doing in the fridge?"

"Cryoincubating. He wasn't supposed to hatch till I warmed him up. What did you do?"

"Soft-boiled him."

"Oh, well. It's okay. I can turn him in early."

"No, it's *not* okay. This is not a pet-friendly apartment."

"Sorry, sorry. I'll get him out of there. He's probably a little premature, so keep him warm till I get back."

"What do you want me to do, simmer him?"

"Perfect. I'll be home in twenty minutes. I promise."
Click.

It was more like forty. In the meantime, I scooted the colander to one side, plugged the drain, re-boiled both kettles, and dumped their contents into the sink. When I removed the colander, the dragon was floating neck deep in the water with his stubby wings spread out like laundry. Little bits of eggshell, cherry tomato peel, and breadcrumb swirled around him.

I sat on the counter. We watched each other.

I'd seen dragons before, but only behind glass. Usually they're green or brown. There's a sanctuary for endangered black ones somewhere in North Wales that I'd visited with Mom and Dad on a UK road trip back in high school. I didn't know they came in red. Maybe it was a juvenile thing.

The front door opened. Aurelia had brought a friend with turquoise hair and a toaster oven on a library trolley.

"Hey!" she said with the bright, desperate grin of somebody who hopes they're not in as much trouble as they think they are. "Marlene, this is Dev. They're in biothaumaturgy with me. Dev, this is my roommate, Marlene. She's Canadian."

"Do you really get moose in your swimming pools in Canada?" said Dev. "I saw this YouTube video once."

"Why didn't you tell me to watch out for the eggs?" I demanded.

Aurelia took her end of the library trolley and maneuvered it through the doorway. When the wheels hit the doorstop, the toaster oven almost jounced off. The plug fell on the floor and Dev ran it over with the back wheels. Aurelia ended up squashed against one end of our ratty sofa. She climbed over the arm. Dev pushed the trolley up against it so they could squeeze in around the doorframe. There was no room to shut the door.

"I forgot about it," said Aurelia.

"You forgot there was a dragon in our fridge?"

"Sorry. Sorry."

"What's the toaster oven for?"

"Incubation. I told you. He's probably premature."

"I'm not hatching mine till the twenty-third," Dev supplied.

I took a deep, calming breath to let both of them know that I was annoyed but choosing to be a good sport. "He's in the sink."

Aurelia went to look. "Oh!" she yelped. "Dev, Dev, come see this! Ah!"

Dev also had to clamber over the sofa. I took the abandoned cart and executed a seventeen-point turn that got it wedged between wall and coffee table so I could shut the door. The only thing worse than a baby dragon loose in our flat would be a baby dragon loose in our building.

"Whoa!" Dev said. "Aurelia, your Canadian didn't say it was red!"

"It's red," I said. "Is that bad?"

"Bad?" Aurelia squeaked. When I joined them in the kitchenette, she was bouncing up and down on her toes while Dev stared at the dracling with what looked like reverence. "Bad? No, it's not *bad*. It's, it's, it's..." She whipped around and threw her arms around me.

"Eek," I said.

"It's, it's, it's..."

"Endangered?" Dev hazarded. "No, not like *endangered,* endangered, more like..."

"*Mythical,*" said Aurelia. "Dev, we hatched a red dragon. I hatched a red dragon. *Marlene* hatched a red dragon." She squeezed me. "You're amazing. Literally, I could bring in, like, a toenail clipping and get an A. I could snooze through my exam and get an A. I owe you, like, a million coffees."

"I know what you can do for me," I said.

"Get the dragon out of the sink?"

"Yes, please."

Dev squeezed past us. "I'll preheat the toaster oven."

"He needs a name," said Aurelia, drifting back to gaze at her red dragon.

"How d'you know it's a he?"

"I could flip him over."

"No, thanks. I'll take your word for it. You could call him Bingo."

"Smaug?" Dev called. I decided I liked them.

"Something Welsh," said Aurelia dreamily. "He's on the flag."

"Cwtch? Araf?" Those were the only Welsh words I knew off the top of my head. Cwtch means hug. It's on all the slate plaques in the gift shops. Araf means slow. It's painted on the road at uncontrolled intersections.

"Something out of the Four Branches," said Aurelia.

I'd taken a Welsh mythology class last semester. The Four Branches of the Mabinogi were the backbone of the *Mabinogion*. They were oral legends written down in medieval times. Aurelia had never actually heard of them till I nerded out to her, but when I gave her my copy, she dutifully read it cover to cover.

"Pwyll," she tested. She leaned over the sink and cooed, "Are you a Pwyll? Who's my Pwyll-boy?"

"Arawn, lord of the Otherworld," suggested Dev. "Aurelia, where's your socket?"

"Behind the sofa," we chorused. Aurelia added, "Rhonabwy? For *The Dream of Rhonabwy*?"

"Only if I can call him Ronny," I said.

"Cei. Culhwch. Pryderi. Are you a *Pryderi*?" she singsonged to the dragon.

"Pryderi reminds me. Have you ever read Lloyd Alexander?"

"No. Who's he?"

"I love *Chronicles of Prydain!*" Dev shouted at the same time.

"Lloyd Alexander's books are the reason I'm here," I said. "He's the reason North Americans have actually heard of your country. Okay, that's it—you, me, popcorn, and *The Black Cauldron* on Friday night."

"No, no, no," Dev said, crowding into the kitchenette behind us. "The movie sucks. You've got to introduce her to the books first."

Aurelia cycled through a few more Welsh names, but it was inevitable. *Lloyd* stuck.

Lloyd the red dragon went into the toaster oven without much fuss. He curled up on the rack with his wings spread out to dry. Aurelia left the door cracked so he could breathe. We were going to have one heck of an energy bill at the end of the month.

Chapter 2: Bidding War

You can always tell when Wales is playing England. Booths with red-white-and-green scarves, Welsh flags on sticks, red dragon plushies, and flag umbrellas sprout on the pavement outside Cardiff Castle, and it's so crowded you can't get within a hundred paces of the stadium or any pub with a telly. Starting at about six p.m., if you want to know who won, all you have to do is open your window. If the drunk fans reeling down the pavement outside are singing the Welsh anthem, they lost. When they win, they'll be off getting drunker in the pubs and bashing the English.

On the day of the Wales–Munster match, I could hear chanting all the way from my archaeology lecture in the Percival building, hours before the doors of Millennium Stadium even opened. When I got out of class, the pavement was flooded with Welshmen with red dragons painted on both cheeks. I almost tripped over a little kid painted red from head to toe. Even the drizzle couldn't dampen the excitement. The streets were gridlocked and there were barriers everywhere. The line at Lidl was so long that I took one look and bought my popcorn at the overpriced convenience store in the student union building. I beat my way back to my apartment. I didn't even know what shape a rugby ball was, but the excitement was contagious.

Aurelia usually got back to the apartment before me, but it was quiet when I keycarded in. Actually, for the last couple weeks, it'd felt quiet even when she was around. There'd been a Lloyd-shaped hole since she handed him over. I reminded myself to be grateful for the Lloyd-shaped hole. I didn't have to waltz with a library cart anymore to get to the kitchenette.

I brewed myself tea and installed myself on the couch to do my archaeology readings. I figured I could finish them before the match if I skimmed. I'd never watched a rugby match in my life. But this one was special, and I'd promised Aurelia.

It'd taken Lloyd a week to outgrow the toaster oven. Aurelia got him one of those doggy jackets at the pet store, but it wouldn't fit over his wings, and he chewed it up anyway. He chewed up her wellies, too. I'd moved all my shoes into my room before he did much worse than frazzle the laces of my hiking boots.

Aurelia skated through the door five minutes before the start of the match. She dumped her soaked backpack on the carpet and dropped onto the arm of the sofa. "Did I miss him?"

I dragged out my laptop and pulled up BBC Wales. They were livestreaming. Practically every news outfit in the country was. I set my laptop on the side table. Aurelia crowded in.

The band was playing the first bars of the anthem. The stadium was packed—tickets had sold out in forty-three seconds, and hardly any of them to Munster fans. The stands were a wash of red and green and white.

"He must be so scared," said Aurelia, crowding me out. Her nose almost touched my screen. She tilted her head like she could get a better angle than the camera's.

"He's not out yet," I said.

"I wish I was there with him."

"He'll be okay."

His arrival was preceded by flares and trumpets. An MP held the leash. Lloyd had put on a few pounds since Aurelia backed him into the cat carrier three weeks ago. He was the size of a Jack Russel terrier. The anthem rose to a crescendo. It was almost drowned out by a roar from the stands. The noise was deafening; even though our apartment was a mile from the stadium, I wasn't sure it was all coming from my speakers.

"He looks lonely," Aurelia said.

"How can he be lonely? He has three million Facebook friends." Welsh Heritage had set up a page for him. It was monitored by a harried intern in an office somewhere who wrote all of Lloyd's posts in lower case. "Anyway," I said, "what's the word on his forever-home? Is the uni still in the running?"

"No, they got outbid. I think it's down to the rugby association and Welsh Heritage," she said. "They're talking about sharing him, but only because Welsh Heritage has a place to keep him and the rugby association has the merchandising machine to promote him."

"Welsh Heritage wouldn't be so bad. Dragons like castles, right?" Cardiff Castle was a huge complex in the middle of the city. There was a Norman motte and bailey, a couple of medieval towers, a whimsical Victorian mansion and a huge reconstructed Roman wall that made a pretty effective dragon pen.

"Yeah," Aurelia said dubiously. "Oh, bless!" Onscreen, a firework had gone off and Lloyd had done an all-four-feet-off-the-ground flinch. He ran in a circle, winding his leash around the MP's legs. She tottered.

"See?" Aurelia said. "He's miserable! He's not a pet."

"Says the girl who tried to put him in a doggy jacket."

"I never should have turned him in. I should've told them my egg was a dud and taken the re-sit in June."

"What would you have done with him?" Dragons grow to the size of crocodiles, not counting the wings, and they don't take to litter training. "It's not like you could've kept him in the apartment much longer."

"I'd take him to Mom's," she said. "Mom has thirty acres on Anglesey. There's lots of room for him to run around, and, and, a creek, and lots of things for him to eat, rabbits and squirrels, I mean, and fish. I swear I've thought this through."

"Okay," I said. "But sooner or later, somebody would notice a big red dragon swanning around Anglesey, and the camera crews would come, and then Welsh Heritage would get involved, and he'd be right back in Cardiff Arena." Because if there was one thing the Welsh had in even greater abundance than sheep and tea, it was nationalism. On Queen Street, the double row of red dragon flags stretched on into the hazy blue. A *real* red dragon was going to attract paparazzi like sheep attract American tourists. "Hey," I added, because she was getting that shimmery look in her eyes, "look at it this way. If Welsh Heritage wins and they put him at the castle, you can go visit him every time you pick up milk." The castle gate was practically in sight of Cardiff Market. "And since you're his hatcher, and everybody knows it—" (and if they didn't, she could show them her BBC interview on YouTube) "—I bet they'll give you a castle key for free."

"What if Cardiff Rugby wins him?"

"Then they'll take him with them for away games, and by this time next year, he'll be better traveled than you and me."

She refused to be jollied out of it. She watched forlornly as the MP led a wobbly Lloyd off the field, trailed by a gaggle of camera crews. The rugby players, spilling onto the field to start the match, looked neglected. I snapped my laptop closed, took one look at Aurelia's face, and offered, "Hot chocolate pity party?"

She burst into tears.

*

The following week, levitating calculators were the least of it. Aurelia couldn't focus. She accidentally turned one of her kettles into a sticky death kettle. Not sticky like it leaves your fingers sticky. Sticky like once you pick it up, you're stuck taking it with you to lecture attached to your hand. She exorcised the shower drain and raised a disgusting hair monster. She woke me up at six in the morning to help her catch and release dust bunnies. Literal dust bunnies, breeding habits and all. There were four when we started. I tossed eighteen outside. It poured all week, so I couldn't even remove myself and my textbooks to Bute Park to do my studying on the grass. I ended up crashing on my Belgian friend's sofa for a couple of nights.

On Friday morning, I swung by the apartment just long enough to jettison my laundry from my backpack and bolt down a piece of bread wrapped around a baby carrot. There was a prosciutto sandwich sitting in the middle of the floor. I wasn't sure if it was an offering to the gods or an appeasement to me, but either way, I didn't know how long it'd been there, so I pitched it. Aurelia must've already left for class.

Running on two hours of bad sofa sleep or not, I wouldn't have missed morning lecture for all the clotted cream in the world. We had a guest speaker. Dr. Gilda Griffith was one of my heroes. If you're not an archaeology major, you don't know her. She's kind of a superstar millennial Indiana Jones, if Indie wore a plaid shirt and turquoise wellies. Look her up. All her documentaries stream on Netflix. I'm not a front-row kind of sitter, but for Dr. Gilda, I sat in the front row.

"Thank you again for coming all the way down here," the regular prof was saying as I settled in. "I know it's not a good time to leave your dig."

"It'll do my interns good to cope on their own for a while," Dr. Gilda said, leaning her elbows on the podium where the mic picked up fragments of her words. "Though when I say I want to let them sink or swim, I don't usually mean it literally." She had an accent that my Welsh friends assured me was "valley." It had a lovely lilt. "We can't do any more digging until the ground firms up, anyway."

She'd set her laptop on the podium. The apple on the back wore a Visigoth suspended votive crown. I had serious decal envy. Mine was a Roman helmet.

The last stragglers took their seats. This was the fullest the lecture hall had been since the start of the semester. I wasn't the only Netflix documentary addict willing to set an alarm and brave the downpour in order to worship at the feet of the brilliant Dr. Gilda.

"Right," she said when the prof gave her the thumbs-up. She jabbed the keyboard. Her first slide was a muddy square pit ringed by waist-high walls. "Let me introduce you to my baby. This is probably the oldest post-Roman fortified residence in Wales. We call it 'Vortigern's Tower.'" She waited a beat. "Yes? No? Anybody? Not even a pity laugh?"

"You all need to read up on your mythology," said our regular prof from his seat at the back.

She sighed. "Kids these days."

That did get a laugh, because she only looked a few years out of postgrad herself. She waved it away. "I'll tell you the story at the end if there's time."

Her topic was the challenges of archaeological survey on unstable ground. The highest corner of Vortigern's Tower was six feet high—for something from the seventh century in a damp climate, that's miracle enough to make an archaeology major fall to her knees and pray—but it was sinking.

"The ground isn't stable," she said. Wide survey shots showed the wind-scraped hillside near Dinas Emrys where the tower was located. "That's slate country," she said. "You've read about hollow hills?

That's what this tower is built on. The problem is that the cave system isn't stable, and neither is the topsoil. The site is more scaffolding than stone now, but we're still losing it."

For the next forty minutes, she walked us through LiDAR scans, underground mapping, anti-erosion efforts, and several funny anecdotes about wrangling with the Welsh Heritage budget office. She'd joked that Vortigern's Tower was her baby, only I could tell it wasn't really a joke. The tower was remote. There wasn't much to see above ground except one corner and some foundations. But the misty hillside was one of those places you could sit alone in the quiet and just keep company with stones that human hands laid fourteen hundred years ago. Maybe that's not a miracle to most people. But to Dr. Gilda it was, and I got it.

I took good notes on my laptop. I jotted down funny professorisms to relay to my parents the next time we Skyped. I surreptitiously searched ways to get to Dinas Emrys by public transit (five transfers, seven hours and fifty-five minutes; forget it). Dr. Gilda was just winding down when a black rectangle appeared in the upper right of my screen.

End call, I clicked, glad I kept my speakers turned down.

The last slide was a loving shot of the tower silhouetted against an amber sunset sky. Dr. Gilda glanced over all our heads at the wall clock. "How are we doing on time?"

"Five minutes," said our regular prof.

"I can talk fast," she said. She rounded the podium and sat on the edge of the lecture stage with her feet dangling. "The oldest stories don't start with *once upon a time.* They just start. This one starts with a king named Vortigern."

The rectangle appeared at the corner of my screen again. The caller ID was "Aurelia in Cardiff." I hadn't known her last name yet when I'd entered her in my contacts. I snapped my laptop shut.

"Vortigern ordered a tower built on a hill," said Dr. Gilda. "Every day, his builders raised the walls, but every morning, when Vortigern came to check their progress, the walls had fallen down. So he consulted his wise men, and they told him that the blood of a child with no father would purify the site."

My backpack started ringing. There's a dance move universally known as "student dives for phone in silent lecture hall." I caught it on the second ring and jabbed the red upside-down phone button. My phone went dead. I put it on silent and reintroduced it to my backpack, embarrassed. The people to either side of me were giving me that guiltily relieved it-could-have-been-me look.

"Anyway," Dr. Gilda said, "Vortigern sent his wise men to scour the land for a child with no father, and—"

My backpack started vibrating noisily against my leg. I dove for it again, hoping I could silence it before anybody noticed. Dr. Gilda trailed off, looking annoyed.

"Marlene," said our regular prof, "if it's an emergency, why don't you step outside?"

My cheeks prickled. I could've turned my phone all the way off, but I didn't want to explain in front of the whole class that the emergency probably had eight legs. I grabbed my backpack by the straps and started picking my way over my seated classmates toward the aisle.

"*Anyway*," Dr. Gilda resumed, "the boy that Vortigern's wise men came up with was Merlin. But our boy Merlin has a good sense of self-preservation. When he's brought before Vortigern, 'O king,' says he—" She was even doing the voices. As the doors of the lecture hall fell shut behind me, I resolved that if it was a spider, it was going down the back of Aurelia's jumper.

You want the end of the story? Google it. In about thirty-six hours, I'd wish I had.

I let my phone ring itself to silence as I stomped down the stairwell. I had an hour before my next lecture. I headed for the canteen. As I handed over a pound coin for a scone, my phone started ringing again. I almost turned it off, just to serve Aurelia right, but the opportunity to yell at her while I was still mad won out. "Aurelia, you got me kicked out of lecture."

I was prepared to be grudgingly gracious in the face of her usual fountain of sorries, but she didn't give me a chance. "I missed the bus," she said.

Something in her tone kept me from hanging up. Nobody should sound that panicked about missing a bus. And nobody who lives that close to campus needs to use buses anyway. Cardiff city buses are overpriced and slow and owned by four or five different private companies, none of whom issue schedules with more than their own routes on them, so figuring out transfers requires a third-party app. Lazy people walk.

So I didn't hang up on her. But that didn't mean I'd forgiven her. "Is there something you want me to do?"

There was a long pause. "No," she said. "I was just stress-calling." Her voice quavered. "The next bus isn't for an hour. I'm going to miss my transfer."

"Where are you going?"

"...Home for the weekend."

I heard the dot-dot-dot, but decided not to ask. "To Llanfairpiggledywiggledy?"

"Yeah." She'd given up trying to teach me how to pronounce her hometown. "I was supposed to take the bus to Bristol Parkway, then take the train from Bristol to Stafford, then take another train from Stafford to Crewe, then take...I forget. I have it written down somewhere."

"But you missed the Bristol bus."

"I read the arrival time as the departure. I've never done this without Mam before."

I heaved a sigh so she'd know exactly how long-suffering her roommate was. Then I set down my backpack and pulled out my laptop. "You can race the bus to Bristol Parkway if you take the train. Let me look up times for you."

"Okay," she said uncertainly.

I let the Trainline app do the legwork for me. "There's a train to Bristol in half an hour," I said. "It'll get you to Parkway by eleven-fifty. When's your transfer?"

"I think noonish," she said.

"D'you know how to get to Cardiff Central?"

"Um..."

"Where are you now?"

"Sophia Gardens."

I looked mournfully at the rain still battering the window. I thought how miserable I was going to be sitting through my afternoon lecture in wet shoes. Then I thought of the time I'd mixed up the arrival and departure times on the first leg of a five-bus odyssey and only made it to Tintagel by the skin of my teeth and the grace of a hotel manager's assistant who drove me the final twenty miles after I missed the last First Kernow bus. That'd been my first long weekend here. It'd given me an ironclad faith in my ability to improvise. Since then, the British transit system had been my oyster.

Besides, I was in a martyr mood.

"Tell you what," I said. "I was going to run by Cardiff Market anyway, and that's practically on the way back from Central. We might as well walk that way together."

"I owe you coffee."

"Iced decaf mocha, yes on the whip, some of those little chocolate shavings on top would be nice." Finding an iced anything in Europe was like finding a unicorn. I closed my laptop. "See you in fifteen minutes."

Chapter 3: Fugitives

As far as I know, there are no gardens at Sophia Gardens. Just a parking lot with rows of XXL parking spots for Flixbus, BlaBlaBus, and Megabus, plus a ticket office. Sophia Gardens sits on the far side of the River Taff, behind the castle.

I'd underestimated the distance. I dispensed with the walking paths and squelched across the vast lawns of Bute Park, slipping and sliding in mud up to my shoelaces. The rain whapped the hood of my windbreaker, which really wasn't up to a deluge of British proportions. Pretty soon my shoulders were wet. I didn't want to know what state the contents of my backpack would be in by the time I got to my second lecture.

I was out of breath and about forty-five seconds late when I skidded down the stairs on the far side of the footbridge. Aurelia was easy to spot: she was the round figure in the rain hat and the salmon-colored vegan leather jacket, cradling an enormous purple backpack in her arms. Her backpack was wearing her raincoat, which means her jacket and scarf were soaked and her diaphanous skirt was a lot less diaphanous than it'd been that morning.

"Hi," she said sheepishly.

"Smooth," I said.

"Sorry."

"If it makes you feel better, I've done the same thing."

Her chin jerked up. Then her face cleared. "Oh. Right. Missed a bus."

"What else did you think I was talking about?"

"Nothing."

My feet were already wet, which impaired my curiosity. "So," I said. "We put you on the train at eleven twenty, you're in Bristol by half past twelve, you catch another train to..."

She dug a soggy receipt out of her pocket. On the back were instructions, or what had originally been instructions and were now a blurry blue smear. "Shite," she said.

"Do you have the information on your laptop?"

"Yeah..."

I looked at her backpack, swaddled protectively in her raincoat. "Probably shouldn't pull it out now. You'll drown your keyboard. Wait till you're on the train."

"I don't know," she said weakly. "This train thing. What if I make it worse?"

"Make what worse?"

"I was supposed to be on the last bus from Crewe to Bangor this evening. What if I make it all the way to Crewe on the train, but miss that transfer? I'll be stranded."

Her tone carried intimations of a short, miserable life as a vagrant sleeping under a train station bench.

I shrugged. "There's YHA hostels, there's Airbnb. Most places, you can put a roof over your head for about what you'd pay for dinner at Spoons."

"How do you find someplace like that?"

"On your phone."

"What if there's no service?"

"Then you find a Starbucks or Caffe Nero and steal their Wi-Fi."

"What if there's no Starbucks?"

"Then you play Clueless Tourist and start asking people."

She still looked uncertain, so I added, "I've goofed up transfers before. It's not the end of the world. You improvise. The most you have to lose is your spare change and dignity." I liked to think there wasn't much that fazed me anymore. Still, I distinctly remembered a time when finding myself stranded in Wadebridge with the sun going down made my hands shake. "Hey, you can always call your mom to come get you, right?"

A pause.

"...Right?" I prompted.

"I wanted to surprise her," Aurelia said.

"Well, hold that option in reserve, then." I pulled my phone out of my pocket. "We've got eleven minutes to get you onto that train. It takes about seven minutes to get to the station at a dead sprint. Yes? No? Are we trying for it, or are we standing here getting wet?"

She wavered for a minute. Then she hiked her backpack up on her hip like a baby. "Let's do it," she said.

We sprinted.

If you ever need to find Cardiff Central, start at the castle gates and walk straight. You can't miss it. Unless there's a giant film crew on Queen Street surrounded by a mob of fangirls willing to brave a monsoon in the hope of being extras. (The two reasons people come to Cardiff: rugby and *Doctor Who.*) We detoured all the way to the cathedral and then cut through Cardiff Market, the Victorian bazaar. That put us back on track.

Queen Street is the nightclub street, and during the day, it has that faintly disappointed air that glamorous places get in daylight. There was no car traffic, and in the rain, no foot traffic either, just mashed-flat Styrofoam takeout cartons and soggy crinkled admission bracelets. Once, I saw an onion skin floating in a puddle here and thought it was a good metaphor for downtown Cardiff. The ranks of Welsh flags hung limply on their poles, the red dragons hiding between folds of white and green nylon. With nobody in our way, we put on a turn of speed that had my backpack jiggling and Aurelia's rain hat skewing sideways on her curls.

"Oh," she panted when I turned us past the modern all-glass hotel and we skidded onto the drive outside the station. "*That's* where the signs were pointing. I always miss that turn."

To be fair, the station's a little hard to see from the corner, because the drive curves and the sandstone facade is at a funny angle. "I had help getting here the first time too."

I could have left her there, but I decided I might as well see her as far as the ticket gate. If anyone was capable of reading a departure board wrong, it was

Aurelia. "The self-service machines are self-explanatory," I said, giving her a prod in the right direction. "I'll just stay here and catch my breath."

Cardiff Central, like most of downtown Cardiff, was a victim of the Luftwaffe. I don't know if the Victorian façade was the original or a reconstruction, but the interior was a slick grayish-white granite. I stationed myself by the sliding doors and peeled off my left shoe. My heel hurt. I was probably going to have a blister. My socks were soaked.

Aurelia was back a minute later. "It won't work," she said.

Contrary to the stereotype, magic and technology get along just fine. Aurelia's problem with the digital world was all Aurelia. I sighed. "Let me see."

The issue, we quickly deduced, was her debit card, which the machine kept spitting back. "Do you have cash in your backpack?" I asked.

"Yes...no...yes." She shifted her backpack uncomfortably on her hip. In all the time since we'd met at Sophia Gardens, she hadn't stopped clutching it in the crook of her arm. "Yes, I do, but I can't get to it. It's, um, buried way at the bottom. Can I borrow twelve pounds? I promise I'll pay you back. With interest."

"Yeah, no problem," I said, anticipating a quiet weekend with the apartment and the wok pan all to myself. I started punching in Bristol Parkway. She had three minutes to get to Platform 6.

"Wait," she blurted before I could press *continue*. "Come with me."

"What?"

"Come meet my mom. Do you like ponies? We have ponies."

"Aurelia, you don't need me to hold your hand. You'll be fine. Your country is half the size of my province. I don't think you could die a lost and forgotten vagrant under a station bench if you tried."

"That's not it," she said. "It'd be fun. Remember how we said ages ago that you should come home with me sometime? Why not now?"

I held up three fingers and counted down. "I have lecture in an hour and a half. I'm not packed. And after six months here, I still can't pronounce your town."

"It'll be an adventure for your blog," she coaxed.

I hadn't touched my blog since Christmas. But I had to admit, with or without Aurelia, Anglesey had been on my list. It was the isle of the druids. There wasn't much there, but it would still be cool to say I'd been.

"Pleeease?" Aurelia made puppy eyes.

I thought about the lecture I'd be missing. The exam wasn't for ages. And I wasn't in a hurry to show my face around Percival till everyone forgot about the phone thing. As for not having packed, my packing list usually consisted of toothbrush, pajama bottoms, clean underwear, and charger. I was fully capable of living out of a purse for three days.

"Two minutes," Aurelia added.

No time for indecision. The quantity box on the screen said 1. "Fine," I said, and hit the plus button. I punched in my PIN. Two tickets printed.

I grabbed my card and the tickets and we pelted through the ticket gate. We ran up the stairs to Platform

6. There was a train waiting there with its doors open. I jumped through. Aurelia hesitated. "Are you sure this is the right one?" She craned her neck to look at the departure board. "Let's look at the ticket one more time just to be sure. Can I see it? There's nothing on the train that says Bristol, is there?"

"It's the right time and the right platform." I had one foot still on the stair. "Come on."

She waffled a few seconds longer. Then a long pneumatic hiss wafted from the engine. She sprang past me just as the doors slid shut. They caught the hem of her skirt. The train lurched slowly into motion. I grabbed the strap of her backpack to free her hands, but she didn't let go, and we did a tug-of-war that ended with her skirt free.

"Thanks," she said breathlessly.

We squeezed down the aisle, lumpy backpacks and all, and snagged seats facing forward. I let her take the window. When we'd both caught our breath, I looked us over. I started to laugh. "We look like we're on the run from the Welsh mafia." My shoes were more mud than canvas and her cap was backward on her head. The rubber buffer on the doors had left two black lines on her skirt where they'd pinched it.

"We're fugitives," she agreed. Her voice quavered, but if she could joke, she must be feeling a little more confident.

I wriggled out of my wet windbreaker as the train rolled from the station. I rested my backpack at my feet so it would stop dribbling water on my jeans. After a moment's hesitation, Aurelia did the same with hers, though her feet bracketed it protectively.

"Let's figure out our route before anybody's phone runs out of battery," I suggested, but her forehead just thunked exhaustedly against the rattling glass, and I was too tired to follow up. For a while, we listened to the chug-chug of the wheels and watched the gray and green countryside blur past.

"Do you have a water bottle?" Aurelia asked after a while.

I unclipped my water bottle from its carabiner and handed it over. "Got a snack?" I asked.

"I have a prosciutto sandwich."

"No, you don't."

"Oh. Shite."

As long as we'd been running, I'd been warm enough. Sitting still in my seat, the clamminess started to get to me. I tried to fold up my cuffs to get the wet fabric off my wrists. I missed my gloves.

To kill time, I opened up my backpack and took inventory. It was a good thing I'd been sleeping at Clara's place the last few nights—I had my toothbrush. Apart from that, my worldly possessions for the weekend consisted of laptop; phone; charging cords; metal water bottle; pair of socks that might've been clean, I wasn't sure; reading glasses; archaeology textbook; headphones; Kindle; and smushed granola bar. Leave it to me to have four potential reading devices but no hair tie. I eyed Aurelia's bulging backpack, wondering whether it might make up the deficit.

It was only because I was watching it that I saw it twitch.

"...Aurelia?" I said slowly. It's a mark of how little hope I held out that the first thing I did was make sure there was nobody else within five rows of us. Only then did I check her feet to see if she was tapping them, and if that might've been what made the zipper dance.

She took a deep breath. "Yes?" she said meekly.

"When were you planning to tell me who you had in your backpack?"

"When you'd dried off and looked warmer."

With some hesitation, I reached down and tugged the zipper open a few inches.

A pair of red nostrils appeared, and then a whole adder-shaped head forced the zipper wider, followed by a snaky neck.

"Oh, no, you don't," said Aurelia, poking Lloyd between the eyes and trying to push him back inside. He wove his head hypnotically, avoiding her.

I couldn't think of any swear words strong enough to express my dismay. "Aurelia, you idiot" didn't come close. I said it anyway, just to get it out of my system. Then I added, "Is he hungry? Will he go back in if you feed him? Please tell me you brought something."

"A prosciutto sandwich," she said in that desperately cheery voice.

"Here," I said, fishing out my granola bar. I unwrapped it and broke off an end. "Lloyd, you want it? You want it? Go get it." I stuffed it past him into the backpack.

Lucky for me, he was gullible. He turned around to rootle for it, and Aurelia pulled up the zipper before he caught on.

"What's he *supposed* to eat?" I said when we'd both stopped clutching our hearts.

"Mice," she said mournfully. "I couldn't do it. I bet you could."

"No way."

"They're smaller than harvester spiders."

"They're cuter, too." I didn't mind the crickets, but I drew my line at mammals. "We can pick up a sandwich for him at Bristol Parkway. Speaking of. I have three questions. How did you steal a dragon? *Why* did you steal a dragon? Oh, God, I'm an accessory to a dragon-napping. Aurelia, you're going to get me kicked out of your country. If anybody asks, I never saw the dragon, I never heard the dragon, I never fed the dragon my granola bar, capisce? As soon as we get to Bristol I'm turning around and going back. No, as soon as we get to Bristol I'm turning around and giving Lloyd to a security guard. Augh."

She was doing the big-brimming-eyes thing again. "He was miserable," she said. "He *hated* being a celebrity."

"Oh, so he's going to retire to an island like Jackie O?"

"Anglesey's an island."

"Don't talk to me. I don't want to be any more complicit. Anything you say, I can and will use against you to get myself out of trouble in a court of law. I don't want to know how you stole a dragon."

Chapter 4: How Aurelia Stole the Dragon

"It was easy," she said. "They've been keeping him at the castle."

"In a dungeon?" I mumbled into my hands.

"No, in the gift shop," she admitted. "He had a doggy bed."

"*I* wouldn't be dissatisfied with life in a gift shop."

"When I came in, there was this five-year-old pulling his tail and saying 'iguana, iguana!'" said Aurelia. She shuddered. She didn't like kids. "I told the volunteer at the ticket window that there was a teenager with a can of spray paint eyeing up the Roman Gate, and she went running out the door."

The Roman Gate is all the way on the other side of the castle, and you can't see it till you've gone around the base of the Norman motte. Aurelia might've had the judgment of a gerbil, but she could be clever in a twisty sort of way.

"Anyway," she said, "then I told the kid and the mom that I was the volunteer who was supposed to take him to the vet, because he had a very contagious skin fungus, and while they ran to the washroom to scrub their hands, I coaxed him into my rucksack and walked straight to Sophia Gardens."

"Aurelia, I don't even know what they're going to charge you with. They'll probably invent something."

She set her chin bravely. "I don't care. If you don't want to come, then don't."

"I won't. Thanks."

We ignored each other for the rest of the journey. I watched the industrial wasteland that is most of south Wales scroll past the window.

It was probably a good thing I was there, because she started to gather up her backpack and jacket at Bristol Temple Mead. I told her to sit down. Silence reigned until the brakes squealed at Bristol Parkway. Fortunately, when we disembarked, the backpack was quiescent.

"You better hurry," I said. "You've got about seven minutes to get to your bus."

Bristol Parkway is one of those huge concrete stations that look like they were cast from a single XXL mold. At the end of our platform, I spotted a bobby in one of those funny bowlers that make British cops look like Charlie Chaplin. He was standing at the end of our platform with his hands in his pockets and his nightstick hanging from his belt. For a few seconds, I thought wildly that news of Lloyd's kidnapping might have run ahead of us. I looked away and pretended to be deeply fascinated by the vending machine. Aurelia spoiled the I-don't-know-her impression by tugging on my sleeve.

"What?" I said.

"I need to buy Lloyd a sandwich."

"Yeah?"

Sheepishly, she said, "My wallet is still under Lloyd. I swear I'll pay you back."

I threw up my hands. "Fine. But then I'm going back to Cardiff. I might still catch the second half of lecture."

We ran to the Caffe Nero near the exit.

"Let's go over your itinerary one more time," I said while we fidgeted in line.

She screwed her face up in thought. "Megabus from Bristol Parkway. It's the Manchester bus."

"Okay."

"Get off in Stafford. Walk to the train station."

"How?"

"Google Maps."

"Attagirl."

"Catch the West Midlands train toward Liverpool. Get off at Crewe."

"That's the tight transfer?"

Defensively, but with fresh confidence, she said, "I'll make it."

"Okay. Then what?"

"The Virgin Trains train to Chester. Off at Chester."

"You've now crossed the England-Wales border twice. What app came up with this cockamamie route?"

"There's an app for that?"

Luckily, we'd just reached the front of the line, or I might have had to strangle her. She grabbed a ham sandwich. I grabbed a tuna one, because I knew in her concern for Lloyd, she'd forget to feed herself. I paid for both sandwiches.

"Okay," I said as she thrust a sandwich into each jacket pocket. "You're in Chester. What now?"

"Transpennine to Holyhead." The triangular plastic containers made the sandwiches stick out at awkward angles. The tuna one looked in danger of falling out. "Off at Bangor."

"Good. What next?"

"There's another bus. It's the, um...I forget the number, but it'll have the name of my town on it."

"Llanfairpiggledywiggledy?"

"Close enough."

"At least at that point your mom probably won't throw you in the Irish Sea if you call her for a ride. Think you can remember all that under pressure?"

She nodded jerkily. The motion made the tuna sandwich start to slide. She caught it and jammed it more firmly into her pocket.

"How about I walk you to your bus?" I suggested. "I have to get a ticket back to Cardiff anyway."

Barring the exit was one of those automatic turnstiles that won't open until you've fed your ticket into the automatic scanner-shredder. I fed mine. The turnstile turned. I waited on the other side for Aurelia.

She stared at the ticket slot like she'd never seen one before.

"Aurelia?" I said. "What's wrong?" I fished my phone out of my pocket to glance at the screen. Two minutes till her bus was set to depart. Looking across the parking lot, I could see a Megabus at the bus shelter.

"I..." she said. "Was I supposed to keep my ticket?"

I covered my face with my hands.

"It'll be okay," she said with slightly flimsy cheerfulness. "I'll do Clueless Tourist to the nice policeman. He'll help."

"You and the dragon in the backpack?"

"Oh, good point." She shrugged out of one shoulder-strap and hoisted Lloyd over the turnstile. "You hold him."

"I wasn't volunteering," I said, but it was too late; I had to catch him or let him fall. I glared at her. "Now I'm not just a witness. I'm actually holding the kidnapped dragon."

"Sorry. Sorry. Sorry. I'll be right back." She bolted back into the station. I held the backpack. Lloyd weighed a ton. I still had my backpack on my back, so I put Aurelia's on forward like a baby sling and settled back to monitor the bus stop. "Just you and me, huh, Lloyd?"

There was a small answering twitch, so at least I knew he hadn't suffocated in there. I wondered if the cold was making him sluggish. Good thing Aurelia wasn't trying to do this in August.

"You know," I told him conversationally (I was talking to a dragon; I must have been feeling frayed), "I've never been an outlaw before. I wonder what Aurelia's profile would look like on *Criminal Minds.* 'The unsub is a female between eighteen and twenty-two with a martyr complex and probable arcane training. She has a high IQ and low self-confidence. Most likely working with an accomplice...'"

Under the overhang, we were perfectly positioned for a front-row view of the bus pulling out.

*

Aurelia was all smiles and sorries as a transit worker in reflective vest scanned his all-purpose card for her and unlocked the turnstile. She came out walking backward, waving to him as he stumped back into the station. I caught her by the shoulders and turned her around to face the empty bus stop.

"Oh," she said, face falling. "Oh, shite."

I handed Lloyd back to her. "So what are you going to do now?"

She squinted at the stop like she thought maybe a spell had turned the bus invisible. In a small voice, she said, "I don't know."

I looked at my phone for the umpteenth time. It was a little after half past. "You know," I told her carefully, "if we got back on a train *right now,* we could make it back to Cardiff by early afternoon. They'll know Lloyd's missing by now, but he'd only have been gone for a couple of hours. I might be persuaded to ask the lady in the gift shop stupid history questions long enough for you to turn him loose on the grounds. It'd just look like he wandered out the door when nobody was watching."

She hugged the backpack closer to her chest, eliciting a squirm that dislodged the tuna sandwich from her pocket. It bounced off her shoe. She chewed her lip. "Maybe," she said slowly, "maybe it's for the best. I don't know why I thought I could do this. I mean—" she gave me a wobbly brave smile, "—I can't even escape a train station. I don't know how I'm going to escape police and a nationwide manhunt."

I retrieved the sandwich and wiped groundwater off the packaging. "That's the spirit. Let's go get tickets back to Cardiff."

"But then again..." She trailed me to the ticket window. I wasn't sure if she was talking to herself, Lloyd, or me. "If I quit now, I'll spend the rest of my semester wondering whether I could have succeeded."

"If at first you don't succeed, destroy all evidence you tried?" I suggested. It was my motto.

I have the five people ahead of us in line to blame for what happened next. I'd talked myself out of Aurelia's madcap adventure, and nearly talked Aurelia out of it, too, but the long line resulted in a three-minute lull in which Aurelia proceeded to talk herself back into it. "But isn't it better to know than to wonder?" she said. "I mean, I think I'd rather know for sure I was a failure, than spend all my time thinking I *probably* was. No, that sounds grim, too. I didn't mean it like that. What I *mean* is, what if I surprise myself? What if we actually make it to Anglesey? I'd never know if I quit now, and Lloyd would spend the rest of his life in captivity just because I thought I couldn't handle a few train transfers."

I sighed. I was getting hungry. I wanted to go back to the apartment and dry off and make myself something hot to eat in the wok.

"Besides," Aurelia rattled on, "I bet Taran and Eilonwy wouldn't quit now."

I blinked. "You actually read *Chronicles of Prydain*?"

"I was curious. I wanted to know what you'd named my dragon after. I liked them. Well, the fourth one had nothing to do with anything. I liked the rest. But the ending is so *sad,* 'cause he never tells you magic came back eventually. Anyway—" she looked at me expectantly, "—heroes don't quit."

"You're trying to be manipulative, but you're not as subtle as you think."

"Don't you want to have a good story when you get home?" she coaxed. "Not every Canadian exchange student gets to help rescue a dragon from a sinister government organization."

"I wouldn't be rescuing a dragon from a sinister government organization. I'd be rescuing a magic major from her own inability to effect a train transfer."

"Exactly," said Aurelia, as if she'd just proven a point. We were almost to the window, but the man in front of us was having trouble with his card. "One way or another," she said with mounting certainty, "I'm going to do this. Come or don't. It's your choice. You decide what you want on your conscience. Oh, look," she chirped, pointing at the departure board above the ticket window. "There's a train straight to Chester. We could cut out the middle steps." She eyed me expectantly as the man in front of us walked away grumbling.

"Can I help you?" asked the bored woman at the window.

Aurelia leaned past me and said, "One ticket to Chester, and..."

They both looked at me.

I wasn't buying the thing about adventures. And I wasn't that worried about Aurelia getting herself and Lloyd to Llanfairpiggledywiggledy in one piece; I'm a big proponent of "When all else fails, call Mom."

The thing is, I wouldn't have got on that first train if I wasn't a little bit interested to see how this was going to turn out. I mean—I had no exams coming up, not much homework to do, and I'd already poked my nose into every castle and old building in a thirty-mile radius of Cardiff. Frankly, by this point in my year abroad, I was bored. If I'd really wanted a dry weekend, I would have texted Aurelia directions to the station and spared my shoes the mud. Going back to Cardiff now didn't make sense. And besides, it's nice to have someone to condescend to.

"Better make that two tickets," I said.

It was just possible, I thought as I watched them print, that Aurelia was exactly as subtle as she thought.

Chapter 5: Wales's Most Wanted

The train was practically empty. We claimed one of those plastic tables that looks like a gray ironing board with rubber edges. We took the seats facing forward and piled my backpack and our wet coats across from us.

A vent blew hot air across our shoes. Aurelia maneuvered her backpack in front of it.

"Are you sure that's a good idea?" I asked.

"I'm cold and your teeth are chattering, and we're warm-blooded mammals."

"I like Lloyd cold. Cold reptiles are slow. Slow reptiles are easy to catch if they get out of the backpack."

"I know. I thought of that." She chewed her lip. "I don't know how cold is dangerous-cold for a juvenile dragon. We didn't study juveniles. Once they hatched, the grad students took over."

I frowned. There was a question that had never occurred to me before. "What happens when the grad students are finished?"

"The sanctuary at Blaenau Ffestiniog takes them on if they're not big enough to fend for themselves yet. Eventually they're released in Snowdonia National Park. The wild population is endangered, you know."

That was a funny thought. Our dragons back home were invasive. My landlady put rocks on the lids of her garbage cans so they wouldn't get in. I had a classmate who found a dead one curled up in his bike pannier. They're everywhere. But those are a skinny, whiskery, non-native species that compete with local wildlife and land people's outdoor cats in the vet's office. *Draco cambrica* hadn't embraced the twenty-first century with the same gusto. Slate mining had destroyed a lot of the caves and hollow hills they lived in, and then there was urban sprawl, etcetera.

The zipper of Aurelia's backpack jingled, reminding me that while I'd been losing an argument, Lloyd had been thawing in front of the vent. "Just don't open the backpack," I said. The only other people in our car were a businessman with his earbuds in and a pair of old ladies with fantastic church hats. None of them had even looked our way when we boarded, but if a dragon the color of a stop sign started running around the car, one of them was bound to notice. "When we're ready to feed him his sandwich," I added, "you should take him into the bathroom and lock the door so he won't run away."

"That's brilliant." Aurelia beamed. "I knew I brought you along for a reason."

We settled into a slightly less prickly silence. I was pleased with my idea and trying not to show it. She was pleased about something, too, probably buying me off with flattery so I didn't keep arguing to leave Lloyd in cryostasis for the duration of the trip. The backpack squirmed happily against the toes of our shoes.

"I wonder if we're felons yet," I said. Putting it like that made the whole thing sound funny.

"Look it up?"

"I'm not sure I want to know." But now that the idea had been floated, I couldn't resist pulling out my phone. The battery was hovering around thirty percent even though I'd barely used it today. It was getting on in years, and cold weather always drained it fast. "Here, pass me my charger, will you? It's in the outer pocket of my backpack."

Aurelia reached across the table and wiggled my charger free while I opened Safari. I wasn't sure what to search for, so I just put in "red dragon breaking news."

"I saw an outlet..." Aurelia said, folding herself awkwardly under the table to search for the plug.

The train was now rolling through marshy western English fields. Hedges and boxy brick farmhouses trundled past our window. The cell service wasn't great. The blue processing bar got three-quarters of the way across the top of my screen and stopped.

"D'you like tuna or ham better?" I asked while I waited.

"Oh, better save the ham for Lloyd." Her head was still under the table. Her voice was muffled. "Shite, I'm going to need your dead phone's flashlight to find the plug to revive your dead phone."

"It's not completely dead." I handed the phone down to her. Her knee mashed my foot. There was a chirrup of protest that could have come from her, my phone, or Lloyd.

"Sorry," she said.

I unwrapped the tuna sandwich. I should've grabbed napkins.

My phone buzzed against the table as the battery in the corner lit up green. "Hah!" Aurelia crowed. She backed into the aisle and straightened up. Her hands were covered in unidentified floor crumbs, which she wiped on her skirt. She dropped into her seat. "Glad you've got your charger," she said, "cause guess whose charger is still plugged into the wall at home?"

That didn't surprise me. "I guess this is a one-phone circus till we get to Llanfairpiggledywiggledy."

"We'll have to work on that," she said. "Come on. Impress my mam. Llan—"

"Shan," I repeated obediently. I couldn't do the Welsh *ll*, not for wont of trying.

"—fair—"

"—fair—"

"—pwyll—"

"—pweesh—

"—gwyn—

"—gwyn—"

"Oh, look, results," I said, and then hissed through my teeth.

"What? What is it?" Aurelia crowded me out. I let her grab the phone. She held it an inch from her nose.

"Lloyd missing—presumed stolen," she read. Her finger flicked down the list of results. "Where is Lloyd? Dragon vanishes from castle; police investigate." Flick. "The Search for Lloyd: Updates on the half-hour." Flick. "Security footage surfaces showing alleged dragon thief.

Shite, that's me. Well, nobody's come forward to ID me, good, and it's pretty blurry." *Flick.*

I rested my face in my palm. "Every policeman in Wales is going to have that photo pretty soon." This was bad. If they got hold of her name, her mom's place was the first place they'd send patrol cars.

She kept reading headlines. "BBC Wales says 'A Dragon Missing, a Nation in Suspense.' The Aberdare Tattler says 'Dragon Heist?' Damn, this thing has a lot of likes—one, two, three, four, five, bloody hell, isn't six zeroes a million? They're organizing a vigil in Bute Park for him. Ugh. Oh, look, Lloyd sightings in, um, Queen Street Arcade, St. Fagan's, Hay-on-Wye, Llanbedr DC..." her voice was getting smaller. She hit refresh and started at the top of the result list. "After Lloyd: What will we do without our national dragon?" Flick. "Cardiff University guest lecturer Dr. Adams presents a special lecture, A Flag Made Flesh: Sociocultural Implications of the Advent and Loss of a National Treasure." Flick. "Who Is Really Behind Lloyd's Mur—murder?!"

"The English?" I guessed.

"Yeah." Flick. "Rumors circulate: Did the Deep Government Abscond with Our Lloyd?"

"Aurelia, those who mind don't matter, and those who matter don't read tabloids."

"That was BBC Wales." She hit refresh. Thankfully for both of us, the train plunged into a tunnel. My last bar evaporated. The screen came up blank.

"Aurelia, you're leaving a nose print on my phone," I said, pinching the top of the phone and trying to wriggle it out of her death grip. She sagged into her seat like an airbag ten minutes after a collision. In the fluorescent train lighting, her face was gray.

Not sure what else to do, I held out her half of the tuna sandwich. Mechanically, she took it.

"What I don't get," I said, "is why everybody is so starry-eyed. Why can't they take a brown dragon and spray-paint it if they need somebody to open the rugby matches? I mean, I get tradition. I wouldn't study archaeology if I wasn't a nut for old stuff. But Lloyd is six weeks old. What do they mean, 'what'll we do without Lloyd'? Exactly what they were doing seven weeks ago, before I hatched his stupid egg."

"I think I get it," Aurelia said in an even smaller voice.

"Get what?"

The train burst out of the tunnel and into a gravel-sided ditch with scrubby trees growing along the top. Telephone lines swooped between their poles overhead like omen birds. "I get the starry-eyed thing," she said. She was still holding the tuna sandwich like she'd forgotten what hands were for. I watched a runny glob of tuna slide down the crust and drop into her lap. "I mean," she said slowly, "I get why Lloyd matters."

"Why?"

"I'm not sure you'll understand."

"Ouch."

"No, I don't mean it like that. It's just, you want history you can hold in your hand. It's not real to you till you know the Marquess of Bute didn't reconstruct it in the 1880s."

Reconstructions were a subject on which I'd vented more than once upon returning to the apartment from a castle trip. The Victorians were the usual offenders. "Okay," I said. "I take your point. I like putting my hand on something and knowing that somebody my age fifteen hundred years ago put her hand in the same spot. It's like my hand is touching hers. That's the only time she's...real."

"Yeah. But all this—" She waved her hand, making *this* encompass everything on my phone, "—is a different kind of real. It's story-real."

"I like stories, though. Myths are interesting. They can tell us all kinds of things about the people who created them."

"No, but that's what I mean!" said Aurelia, waving the sandwich. "You're still about the *real.* The stuff behind the myths. That's not the point."

There was a pneumatic cough as the doors at the far end of the car opened. A man in flat cap and waistcoat shuffled through, armed with satchel and hole-puncher. I dug out my ticket. "This conversation got really existential," I said.

"Sorry, sorry."

"If you're back to apologizing, I guess you must be feeling more like yourself."

She patted her pockets. Then she bent down to pat her backpack.

I closed my eyes. "So much like yourself that you misplaced your ticket?"

"I swear I had it!"

The ticket inspector was bending over the teenager. I tapped Aurelia on the shoulder. I fanned myself casually with the two tickets, waiting for her to straighten up and notice, but she didn't. In a tiny voice addressed to my shoes, she said, "Shite."

"What?"

"Come on, Lloyd," she said. "Who's my Lloyd-boy? Let's just wriggle right back where you came—ow."

"You okay?"

"My fault. I think I poked him in the eye. I can't see a thing. Here, take my sandwich for a sec."

I set her half of the sandwich back in the packaging with mine. I grabbed my phone and flipped on the flashlight. "Here," I said, shining it under the table. I kept one eye on the ticket inspector. I was prepared to tell him we were searching for a dropped earring. Just as long as he didn't offer to help us look. Maybe it'd better be a dropped earplug. A used one. I put both tickets on the edge of the table like an invitation to punch them and pass by. "How's the light?" I asked.

"A little to the right."

I angled the flashlight to the right.

"Sorry, sorry," she said. "My right, not your right."

"Aurelia, we're facing the same direction."

"Left, then. Here, hand me your coat. I'll just drape it over him."

I didn't have room to stand up, because Aurelia was on the aisle side. I folded a foot under me so I could stretch across the table. My windbreaker was balled under my backpack. I tried to tug it free. The backpack tipped.

"Crap!" I said, grabbing for it too late. "Incoming." I kept hold of the strap, but couldn't stop the backpack from thumping to the floor.

"Ow," said Aurelia again, and there was a distinctly Lloydlike cheep of protest.

"Sorry," I said. I glanced at the inspector to see if he'd noticed. He was chatting with the old ladies now. I tried to drag my backpack back onto the table. "It's caught on something," I said. "What's it caught on?"

"Not me," said Aurelia. "Oh, wait, it's snared up with your coat now...just let go. Lloyd's not going anywhere."

I let go and dropped back into my seat, careful not to kick Aurelia or Lloyd as I got both feet back under the table. The inspector was walking toward us. Aurelia wriggled out into the aisle. The sleeve of my windbreaker followed her, caught in the zipper of her boot.

The inspector was a dapper old guy with an ironed handkerchief sticking from his pocket. He looked like somebody who'd be punching the train tickets of the Pevensie kids right before their train dropped them off in Narnia. "Oh, dear," he said cheerfully, looking down at Aurelia. "Tangled, are we?"

"She lost an earring," I said, at the same time that Aurelia said, "I dropped my ticket."

"Is *that* what you were looking for?" I improvised, because both tickets were sitting there on the edge of the table. "You should've said."

Aurelia planted herself cross-legged on the carpet and dug her fingers between her leg and boot. "Marlene, your coat *really* likes me." There wasn't much slack, so she couldn't get the sleeve unstuck. It looked like the Velcro tab at the wrist had attached itself to the lining of her boot. Trust Aurelia to manage that. She was having trouble peeling it up. "I don't want to tear anything," she said apologetically to the inspector, whose way she was blocking.

I scooped up our tickets and held them out to him, hoping it'd keep him from "helping." Absently, he took them from me and punched them. "Need a hand, ma'am?"

"Oh, no, I'm all right," Aurelia said airily.

"Nothing breakable under there, is there?" He bent down, seized the sleeve, and dragged.

What slid reluctantly out from under the table was a knot consisting of Aurelia's purple backpack, my blue one, Aurelia's yellow raincoat, and Lloyd in all his scarlet unsubtle glory. Lloyd's claws skimmed lazily over the carpet. His tail was twined in a Celtic knot with the straps of our backpacks. He looked disinclined to free it. I wondered if he was still cold or if I'd brained him with the falling backpack.

"Crap," I said.

"Shite," said Aurelia.

Lloyd's forked tongue flicked dazedly over the ticket inspector's shoelaces.

I scrabbled for any story to the tune of *this isn't what it looks like.* For the moment, the inspector was staring aghast at Lloyd, whose jaws were working at some tidbit he'd found on the floor, but as soon as he looked at Aurelia, he was going to see a girl whose face was splashed all over the headlines.

"You know," he said faintly, "I've never seen one that color outside the *Hobbit* trilogy. Underrated movies, those." He handed me back the punched tickets. He was still staring. "That's his natural color, is it?" Then, suddenly, he snapped out of it. He expanded with indignation. "Young lady—" he sputtered, "that does *not* look like a regulation pet carrier!"

I blinked. "Oh, um, I, we—"

"—couldn't get him into it this morning," Aurelia inserted.

"Yeah," I said. "Ever try to get a cat into a carrier to go to the vet?"

"It's like wrestling a really pissed-off thornbush," said Aurelia. "Only you can hurt it if you're not careful."

"He shredded my sweater," I added for verisimilitude.

"Look what he did to my hand!" said Aurelia, a little hysterically, and held up a hand that was, in fact, stamped with a little dotted line in the shape of Lloyd's upper jaw. "But really, he's very well-behaved."

"And, and, and, too cold to go anywhere," I stammered. "Look, he's half-hibernating." I gave him a gentle nudge with the toe of my sneaker. Lloyd turned incuriously to investigate, lost interest halfway there, and lay his head down on the carpet. He closed his eyes.

The inspector held up his hands, fending us off. "There's a hefty fine for transporting a pet without a proper carrier, you know."

"Sorry, sorry, sorry, sorry, sorry," said Aurelia. "I'm sorry. I didn't know that. We can get off at the next station."

We can? I thought.

"Really, it's okay," she said. "I mean, it's cold, but if I wrap him really well in my raincoat, I don't *think* it'll be dangerous for him. We can call an Uber to take him the rest of the way to the reptile vet. I mean, I think if we just eat ramen and water for the next month, we should be able to cover the bill and still make rent—"

The inspector's indignation deflated a little. "Well, I'm not sure that's necessary—"

"Marlene can wrap her coat around him, too," said Aurelia. "I mean, I do worry about him a little bit. With the traffic, it'll take longer to go by Uber than by train, but I don't think it's that urgent; he started turning this color, like, late last night, and it's not till they're completely black that the condition's *really* dangerous..."

"Now, really, young lady, I think I can let it slide, just this once."

"Oh, no, I really couldn't let you break the rules for us." She was already gathering her raincoat.

"Stay here," he said. "Please. Let me go speak to the engine room. I'll see if I can get them to turn up the heat. Just—stay." He made a little calming gesture, turned, and walked quickly back the way he'd come. The doors swished open and shut.

I looked at Aurelia. She looked at me. I was bemused; she was exultant.

"English," we chorused.

I guessed we'd be okay until the English channels picked up the story. Or till we crossed back into Wales.

Chapter 6: Thawing the Dragon Was a Really Bad Idea

Aurelia's raincoat was still damp, so she wriggled out of her jacket and draped that over Lloyd. He promptly fell asleep, went limp, and spread out across both our laps. Now that I saw him out of the backpack, I realized he was longer than I'd thought, easily twice the size he'd been when he left our apartment. He must have been in that lanky adolescent phase. His head ended up on my knee and his tail trailed across the aisle. I draped my coat loosely over it, but my prediction about the English held true: either they hadn't seen the news yet, or they just weren't interested. One of the old ladies got up to use the toilet and stepped over his tail like it was nothing more sinister than a cord.

As the train chugged across Worchestershire, the space under the table got noticeably warmer. Air was pouring out of the vent at a rate that made me kick off my shoes and attempt to blow-dry my wet socks. Our window fogged up.

"You know, Aurelia," I said finally, "I'm not sure you really needed me here. If you'd got off at the wrong stop, you probably could have talked your Uber driver into taking you all the way to Anglesey for free. He'd probably stop at a chippie on the way to buy fish for Lloyd."

"I don't know where this is coming from," she said, waving vaguely down at herself so that "this" encompassed everything she'd done since waking up that morning. "Sheer adrenaline, I think."

"If this is you on adrenaline, I don't want to know what the crash will look like."

I was teasing, but her face fell. "*That's* why you're here."

We ate our sandwiches. Lloyd's catnap lasted all the way across Worcestershire. We were somewhere in the West Midlands, a patchwork of green and brown fields bordered by scrubby hedges, when I glanced at my phone and realized the battery was down to 9% and not green anymore.

"Huh," I said. It was still plugged in, but obviously hadn't been charging. I reached under the table and patted till I found the plug. My first thought was that Aurelia had knocked it loose while she was fumbling around down there, but I took it and jammed it firmly into the socket and the battery symbol on my screen still didn't light up. I got a sinking feeling as my fingers traced the cord back toward my phone. It didn't take long to find the bare wire. I pulled the plug and reeled it all onto the table. The middle of my charging cord was tattered white rubber and exposed copper. I groaned. "Lloyd."

"What happened?" said Aurelia. Then she saw. "Oh," she said in a smaller voice. "Sorry," she added.

Lloyd dozed peacefully on. He had one of those baby-animal faces that was angelic in sleep.

I turned my phone off to conserve battery. No phone meant no Google Maps. No Google Maps meant we might have to read a printed train schedule. And we were both children of the 21st century. I could read a route generated by my phone; I wasn't as confident about a spreadsheet full of train numbers and departures rendered in 24-hour military time. I supposed I'd better be ready with my lost-tourist impression.

Aurelia curled over Lloyd and rested her forehead on the table. I dragged my damp archaeology textbook out of my backpack. There were still two hours between us and Chester. I figured I could at least make some headway on my class readings.

We'd just pulled out of Birmingham when the tip of Lloyd's tail started to swish. We didn't have the car to ourselves anymore: the teenager was long gone, but a pregnant mom and a toddler had taken over his table, and a husband and wife armed with a map and speaking German had settled closer to the doors. A guy our age stepped over Lloyd's tail with exaggerated care as he hand-over-handed down the aisle and claimed a seat.

It was a few minutes later that Lloyd started to make quiet smacking noises. His tongue slithered out between his fangs and tasted the knee of my jeans. His eyes stayed closed, but pretty soon the tips of his wings were fluttering.

"Ow," mumbled Aurelia into her hands—he'd flexed his back claws like a cat, and her skirt wasn't much protection.

"Maybe we should start thinking about putting Lloyd back in the backpack," I said. "I mean, before he's conscious enough to protest. We'd better have him out of sight before we cross back into Wales."

At the word *backpack,* both his sets of eyelids slid open.

"Good point," said Aurelia. She hooked a strap with her foot and tried to draw it into her own reach. The movement jostled Lloyd, whose head lifted from my knee. He turned to look at her with a slightly betrayed expression.

"Good boy," I said, petting the back of his head. "Don't mind us. Nothing to see here. Go back to sleep. *Rock-a-bye, reptile, in the treetop... When the vent blows, the cradle will rock... When the bough breaks, the reptile will fall... And solve all my problems, skipped lecture and all..."*

"Marlene!" protested Aurelia.

"What? He can't understand me. Who's the smelly reptile monster?" I cooed. "Who's the horrible, cold-blooded, stress-eating nuisance? Why didn't my cord zap you, hmmm? I liked you better when you were hypothermic."

Lloyd, soothed by my tone, settled his head back on my knee. One set of eyelids slipped shut, filming his eyes. Unfortunately, it was the translucent set. I was pretty sure he'd still see the backpack coming.

"Put your bag in front of the vent for a while," I told Aurelia. "Maybe if we warm it up enough, he'll climb in voluntarily."

"Good idea," she said. She propped her backpack against the wall. It cut off the warm air that'd been blowing across my wet feet for the last two hours.

I wasn't sure exactly where the England-Wales border was. The train drew into Wolverhampton and then out. The only addition to our train car was a young woman in a hijab who looked curiously at Lloyd before settling at the back of the car with her laptop. I risked turning on my phone long enough to look up our next stop.

"Is Shrewsbury in England or Wales?" I asked.

"England," said Aurelia.

"Okay. Operation B-A-C-K-P-A-C-K commences after Shrewsbury."

"Mmph," she said. I was pretty sure I was looking at adrenaline crash. I went back to my textbook. I got most of the way through the chapter on Mortimer Wheeler, but I didn't take in much. It was starting to look like we might actually pull off this dragon heist. We'd arrive in Chester in plenty of time to patch ourselves back into Aurelia's original route. We'd catch a TransPennine in the direction of Holyhead and get off at Bangor. From the harbor of Bangor, you could practically toss a rock across the Menai Strait and hit Anglesey. At that point it might not even be worth searching for the bus. It'd take all of fifteen minutes for Aurelia's mom to come pick us up.

Assuming either of us had a phone functional enough to call her. I supposed if all else failed we could walk the rest of the way; it'd be a hike, but probably a scenic coastal one. I drew a smiley face in the fog on the window to check the weather. The rain had quit sometime in the last fifty miles. The overcast was thinning out. I could see a silver smudge where the sun was trying to burn through.

I dragged myself back to my textbook and got halfway through the case study before the train decelerated into Shrewsbury. I put a hand down to test Aurelia's backpack, which had gotten obligingly warm. My fingers wandered over the zipper. I yanked my hand back. "Ow."

Aurelia mumbled something vague about metal and heat conduction. Well, if boiling water hadn't bothered Lloyd, I didn't think the zipper was going to faze him.

I peered at him. He still only had the translucent eyelids closed, but he was reassuringly limp across both our laps. I wondered if we could just slide him into the backpack like laundry. Without jostling him, I tapped Aurelia on the shoulder. "Are you still conscious?"

"Yeah." She straightened. She rubbed her eyes with her fists. "Is it time?"

"Let's wait till we're moving again. I don't think we should do anything till there's no chance the train doors are open."

"Good thought. Hang on—I have an idea." She produced the ham sandwich from the pocket of her jacket. She peeled up the plastic. "Bribery," she explained. "We'll hold it in reserve."

"My mom says raising kids is all about bribery."

"My mom says the same thing about raising ponies."

"What's your mom going to say about raising a dragon?"

"Expletives."

The train shuddered and pulled away from the Shrewsbury platform. Next stop, Chirk. I looked at Aurelia. She looked at me.

"Now?" I said.

Careful not to jostle Lloyd, she dragged the backpack in front of her knees. She propped it open. "Okay."

We both rested our palms on Lloyd's ribs. They rose and fell peacefully. "Ready?" I said.

"Set."

Lloyd's muscles bunched.

"Push!" I said.

Lloyd exploded straight into the air. A wing slapped me in the face. Aurelia squeaked as his clubbed tail snagged her scarf. A flurry of wings, like a whole flock of pigeons taking off, filled the car. Heads turned. The Germans exclaimed and the girl in the hijab yanked off her headphones.

Lloyd's wingspan-to-baby-fat ratio wasn't anywhere near airworthy. He described a parabola over our heads and came down in the empty seats two rows ahead.

"Shite!" Aurelia exclaimed, springing up. She tripped over the backpack. I couldn't get into the aisle till she was out of my way. In the time it took us both to get free, Lloyd vanished under the seats. A leathery scrabble marked his progress. The mom shrieked and jerked her toddler into the air.

"Nobody panic!" Aurelia cried.

The glass-and-plastic doors at the end of the aisle brought Lloyd up short. They were motion-activated, but the sensor must've been aimed higher than a foot off the carpet, because they stayed shut. Lloyd flopped in a panicky circle, his tail whipping around like a lash.

"Aurelia, don't!" I said as she charged down the aisle ahead of me with her arms outstretched. I grabbed the ham sandwich. "I have an idea! Stop!"

I could see what was going to happen right before it did. Lloyd might not have been tall enough to set off the motion sensor, but Aurelia was. She was still five feet from him when the doors hissed open. The clatter and grind of the wheels on the track rushed into the car, unmuffled. Lloyd shot into the dark accordion-walled passage between cars.

Aurelia halted between the open doors. "Shite," she said. "Sorry."

I caught up. "It's okay. Don't move. I like your bribery plan." I pinched the sandwich out of the package and did a little sandwich surgery. I handed her the bread. She squeezed into the first row of seats so I could crouch on the carpet. I held out the ham and wiggled it temptingly.

The good news was that to open the second set of doors, you had to hit a button at hip-level. Lloyd was pretty well cornered as long as nobody opened them from the next car. The bad news was that by shunting Aurelia aside, I'd just volunteered myself for dragon-grabbing duty. Well, as long as his mouth was full of ham, he couldn't bite me. "Lloyd," I cooed, "come get the yummy ham. Here it is. Come get it."

He was coiled defensively at the foot of the doors. The passage between the cars was loud—the synthetic leather accordion-walls didn't do much to muffle the clatter of the wheels, and the floor was two plates of corrugated iron that swiveled as the train rounded a curve. His eyes tracked the ham, but he had all paws on one plate and he'd backed up so close to the doors that his tail folded under him. Having sprung across that tectonic rift once, he looked like he didn't intend to repeat the mistake. Floors that moved in two different directions must've been a novelty.

"Here, Lloyd," I cooed. "Attaboy." I waved the ham to waft the smell to him. "You know you want it, you overgrown gecko. Come get it."

His tongue flicked, tasting the air. All he'd eaten today had been a piece of granola bar.

"How's it coming?" Aurelia asked, hovering behind me.

"We're coming along just fine," I said in the same soothing voice. "Aren't we, Lloydbucket?" I was going to have to grab him, I could tell. Maybe I should lead with the backpack. "Aurelia, can you bring your bag for me?"

She was looking over my head. There were windows set in the top halves of the doors. From Lloyd's eye level, I couldn't see what she could, but I heard her say "Uh-oh."

I turned "What's going on?"

She waved a hand in front of her throat and mouthed "Abort! Abort!" at the glass, just before the doors hissed and slid open.

Lloyd whipped around so fast his tail almost knocked the ham out of my hand. He tried to propel himself through the doors and instead ran headfirst into a sheer plastic cliff. There was a solid *thunk* that made it scoot back an inch on its wheels.

"Oh!" exclaimed the middle-aged woman on the other side. She craned across the top of her drink cart, trying to see past the canisters of coffee and hot water, the boxes of tea, and the stacks of candy bars and packets of crisps. She looked horrified. "I'm so sorry. Ohmygod. Is she okay?" She looked between me and Aurelia, confused. "I don't hear any crying. Is she okay? Ohmygod."

There was a muddled pause. Lloyd was bobbling his head, more surprised than hurt. It occurred to me that he had about the body mass of a toddler at the early crawling stage.

"Sorry," said Aurelia. "Sorry. Sorry. It's not a kid, don't worry."

"And he brought that on himself, so I wouldn't feel bad," I added. "Just—don't move the cart." I was starting to chicken out about grabbing Lloyd with bare hands. "Aurelia, do you want to do the honors, or do you want to grab the backpack?"

Lloyd picked that moment to recover well enough to waddle a few steps back. It brought him into the drink cart lady's line of sight.

"Augh!" she exclaimed in the same tone one might use for a harvester spider in one's bathtub at four in the morning.

Lloyd's muscles started to bunch.

"Uh-oh," Aurelia said again.

"Watch out," I warned, right before Lloyd sprang. His wings flapped against the accordion walls. He might not have been airworthy, but a parabola was exactly the right flight trajectory to land him in the middle of the drink cart. Tea bags and Mars bars flew everywhere. The drink cart lady screamed bloody murder and leapt back, which cleared the way handily for Lloyd to slither off the cart on her side. One of the coffee canisters did a slow-motion topple after him, and the *thud* when it hit the carpet made the whole floor shake. He disappeared under the seats.

The computerized female voice on the intercom drifted over the chaos:

"Now entering Wales. The next stop is: Gobowen."

Chapter 7: The Fox, the Hen, and the Bag of Corn

Chasing Lloyd wasn't an option—the cart was in the way. At this point, Aurelia didn't look like she'd be above grand theft drink cart, but the canister of coffee was still rolling around on the other side, and the drink cart lady was raking her fingers through her hair and chanting "Ohmygod, ohmygod, ohmygod." To make matters worse, Lloyd had picked the fullest car in the train to launch himself into. I could track his progress by the chorus of startled yelps and the sets of feet flying into the air as he passed beneath the seats. A little old lady yowled in outrage and hoisted her purse over her head like he was after her change. Phones were out. So much for low profile. A small piping voice shrieked "Kitty!"

As far as I knew, trains didn't have security guards. I didn't want to test the theory. "Aurelia, do something," I said. Lloyd held the riveted attention of everybody who'd just had something scaly run over their feet, but a few pairs of eyes were starting to turn in the direction of his source, which was us.

Aurelia cleared her throat. "Um—hi," she said.

"Tell them not to trip the other doors," I whispered.

"Nobody panic," she said loudly. "He's very friendly, and anyway, his neck's too small to swallow anything important."

Passengers were crowding in on our side of the cart, too. The girl with the hijab breathed down the back of my neck as she tried to get a photo over my shoulder.

"Sorry, sorry, so sorry for the inconvenience," said Aurelia, her ingenuity apparently tapped out. I could tell she was going through the same thought process I was, which was that pretty much all the aisle seats were occupied, so to get past the cart, we'd have to get the cart to the place where the aisle widened out for the luggage rack, but that was right in front of the far doors, which would trip the motion sensor and open them. It was basically the riddle of the fox, the hen and the bag of corn.

So far, the court might have me on mild abetting, but active aiding was debatable. I held my breath, waiting for Aurelia to come up with something clever that I could abet.

A man in a button-down got out of his seat to comfort the hysterical drink cart lady. They didn't look like they were going to move out of our way anytime soon. I could only hold my breath so long. I ran out of oxygen before Aurelia came up with anything.

"If we can't get the cart forward," I whispered, "we'll have to pull it back toward us."

"Oh. Good idea."

The push rail was on the other side, and it was hard to get enough traction on the smooth countertop to drag the cart over the door lintel. I managed it by hooking a shoe behind one of the wheels. It clattered loudly on the metal floor between cars. The girl with the hijab shuffled back to make room for us. "What are you guys?" she asked.

"Welsh Heritage volunteers," said Aurelia, at the same time that I said, "International dragon thieves."

She looked like she wasn't sure whether to laugh or take our photo for the police.

I sidestepped into an empty row. Aurelia dragged the cart past me. I stepped back into the aisle. It was her turn to slide into an empty row. I pushed the cart past her. We were both free. That had taken an inordinate amount of brainpower. I pushed the cart past our original seats so I could grab both our backpacks. Then we raced back into Lloyd's car.

The uproar had only spread, so it was impossible to tell which shrieks were Lloyd-induced and which were just part of the general pandemonium. It looked exactly like what happens when one girl in the lecture hall sees a spider on the floor and screams and suddenly everybody who's afraid of spiders, bees, or mice is looking around frantically wondering where and what it is and whether someone else will kill it. Feet were on seats; babies were in the air. A mop dog in a carrier yapped.

"Where is he?" Aurelia cried.

Nobody paid her any attention. She took a deep breath. Then she clapped. It was the teacher clap: *Clap, clap-clap, clap, clap...clap-clap.* Out of sheer ingrained reflex, every head under the age of thirty-five turned our way.

Now that she had their attention, she didn't know what to do with it. "Um...sorry," she said. "Who *actually* has a dragon under their seat at this moment?"

A few hands rose. None of them were near each other.

I got down on hands and knees to look. It was dark under the seats, and I couldn't see very far, because there were bags and feet in the way. Crawling on hands and knees down the aisle would very definitely be aiding, so I didn't. "I'll guard the far door," I said. "You work your way toward me. We'll flush him."

"Brilliant."

It was a good thing I wasn't prone to stage fright, because the whole train car was watching us. I stood by the luggage rack, ready to field Lloyd or make throat-cutting gestures through the glass at anybody who tried to open the door from the other side.

But Lloyd wasn't there. Aurelia reached me. We shared a dismayed look.

"Where's the drink cart lady?" I asked suddenly.

One of the teenagers supplied, "She took that jug of coffee and left."

Aurelia's head dropped into her hands. "Augh," she said. "He could be anywhere by now."

"Anywhere between here and the engine," I said.

Nobody had seen him leave. He must've slunk out behind the drink cart lady while everybody was looking under their seats. *Crap.*

"Can you dowse him?" I asked Aurelia, remembering her thaumocaching unit and how she'd had me hide one of her house slippers in Bute Park so she could practice tracking things down.

"I don't have any of my equipment," she said. "I don't know how to dowse without a learner's rod."

"You can't Google instructions? It's got to be on Reddit."

"I guess," she said.

I gave her my phone. "I'll start looking," I said. "You see if you can figure out how to do a DIY dowse. I bet he's shed a few scales in your backpack, if you need DNA or whatever."

"Okay."

"Best case scenario, I flush him back toward you and we never need a dowser."

"What's the worst-case scenario?" she asked.

"Better not go there."

We split up. I'd lost the ham in all the confusion, and I didn't want a dragon on top of my laptop in my backpack, so I figured if I found Lloyd, I'd try to shoo him back toward her.

We pulled in at Gobowen. Doors hissed open up and down the length of the train. That, of course, raised a whole new worst-case scenario, which was that Lloyd got off without us, but when I felt the blast of cold damp platform air, I figured off the train in this weather was the last place he'd want to be. Embarking and disembarking passengers clogged the aisles. I took a seat and tapped my heels while I waited for everybody to get settled. The train shuddered back into motion.

If I'd known the train had a dining car, I would've saved myself a lot of peering under seats and attracting funny looks. It was the third car behind the engine, and it created a buffer between the plush first-class carriages and the sticky plebeians. Its doors opened on a waft of instant coffee. That was the only identifiably biodegradable smell. Everything else they sold was wrapped in at least one layer of plastic. I stepped inside and walked face first into my worst-case scenario.

My worst-case scenario was sitting on a plastic stool. My worst-case scenario was wearing a Transit Wales vest and a serious-looking metal name badge that said JONES. My worst-case scenario was dangling a strip of cold bacon and apparently teaching Lloyd "sit up and beg." I froze in the doorway.

Officer Jones was a big-bellied Santa Claus type. He had a nightstick in his belt and a pair of stomping shoes, and looked fully capable of apprehending a dragon-napper and her accomplice and marching them off the train at the next stop. If I'd been wondering whether British trains had security guards, here was my answer.

Lloyd snapped the end of the bacon and worried it. Officer Jones laughed. He let Lloyd bite off an inch.

"Can I help you, miss?" said the young guy behind the snack counter, who had a much less serious-looking name badge that said Rajesh.

Officer Jones looked my way. I started to sweat. I was about to throw myself on his mercy and swear that I hadn't known about the dragon till we were underway. I opened my mouth. What came out was, "Tea, please."

"Sugar? Cream?" said Rajesh.

"Yes, please," I said. I had to play it cool.

"One pound, please."

I dug out my debit card. Rajesh stuck it in the machine. I couldn't take my eyes off Lloyd. The greedy little red mercenary hadn't even glanced at me. His eyes tracked the bacon. He had the droopy paw part down pat.

Officer Jones saw me staring. "We're still working on the whining," he said cheerfully.

"Miss?" prompted Rajesh. I realized he was holding out the card reader. I took it. I put in my PIN. I held it out.

"Your card?" he prompted.

"Oh, right. Right." I took my card back.

"Want to pet him?" said Officer Jones.

"He bites," I said reflexively. Then added, "...Doesn't he?" And then, "...She?"

"He's a he," said Officer Jones. "His name's Lloyd. He doesn't need much introduction around here."

"Oh, really? I'm not from around here." I had to warn Aurelia.

"Where's home for you?" he asked.

"Vancouver," I said. "British Columbia. Canada."

"Beautiful place. I've seen pictures."

"Uh-huh."

"Your tea, ma'am," Rajesh prompted.

I took the paper cup mechanically. Train tea is vile and watery. I already knew that. I sipped anyway and scalded my tongue. The cup was too full to walk with. I had to set it down on the counter, and then, because I couldn't abandon it without looking suspicious, I had to sit on a stool.

"Tourist, are you?" said Officer Jones.

"Yeah," I said. I wasn't as fluent a liar as Aurelia. I didn't think it was ethics so much as a lack of creative flair.

"Where are you headed?" he asked.

"Conwy," I said, because it was vaguely in the right direction. "There's supposed to be a really spectacular castle and one of the longest intact city walls in Europe."

"Oh, yeah, there is," said Officer Jones disinterestedly. He dangled the bacon again. "What do you think of Wales so far?"

I blew desperately on my tea. "Oh, I love it here," I said honestly. "There's so much history everywhere. I mean, you can't walk a hundred feet in a straight line without tripping over a wall older than my country. Back home, living history is your seventy-year-old grandma."

"Uh-huh," he said vaguely, giving me the glazed look of a Brit for whom castles are old news. "You want some real living history, here's some right here." His gesture dipped the bacon into reach. Lloyd snapped it up. Officer Jones yanked his fingers back, laughed, and took the bread off the top of his packaged sandwich. There was no meat left on it, so he peeled up the tomato and dangled that. "You've seen our flag?" he said.

"You can't walk far in Cardiff and *not* see it," I said. It's all up and down Queen Street, all over the castle, in all the tearoom windows. It's on the souvenir mugs at the Tim Horton's and the T-shirts in the gift shops. "I like it," I added, and then, to maintain my cover, "Your dragon looks like he stepped right off it."

"Oh, he's not mine," said Officer Jones.

"Really?"

"Funny story." He looked like he relished having a foreigner to tell it to. "Lloyd here, he's one of a kind. There's been no red dragons in Wales in a hundred years."

Roughly fifteen hundred, actually.

"Then along comes Lloyd," he said. "Some uni student reading magic at Cardiff hatched him." He was warming to his theme like a true raconteur. "I guess she must have got attached to him, because she couldn't let him go. He was supposed to become national property—"

Well, sort of; Welsh Heritage was national-ish, I supposed. I wasn't sure about the rugby team.

"But on the eve of his inauguration," said Officer Jones, "the same magic girl comes along and snatches him. It's broad daylight. She storms the castle, tells the volunteers to get lost or she'll hex them, stuffs the poor tyke into a rucksack, and runs."

"Oh?" I said.

"Well, who knows what torments our national treasure suffered," he went on. "But he's safe now. Aren't you, boy?"

Lloyd wasn't nearly as interested in the tomato. He snuffled around Officer Jones's shoes in case any bacon crumbs might have fallen.

"In fact," said Officer Jones, lowering his voice, "stick around, and you might get to see a criminal apprehended."

"Really?" I said, blowing desperately on my tea. I had to escape. I had to get to Aurelia before he did.

"Yes," he said. "I've called ahead to every station along the route. There'll be police waiting on the platform wherever she comes off. How far are you going?"

"Um—Chester."

"Oh, good. You'll get to see it, no matter what happens."

Crap. Wrong answer. If I'd said the next stop was mine, I could've got away. "Okay," I said, trying to think. I hazarded a slurp of tea that made my scalded tongue feel like sandpaper. The train was beginning to slow. "Where are we now?"

"Chirk," said Officer Jones. "The platform will be on the left. Go on—I'll watch your tea."

I had no choice but to go to the window and pretend to look out. We were decelerating into the outskirts of another collection of brick boxes in a rolling green countryside. The hills were getting steeper and higher here, a sure sign that we were moving north. "What about the dragon?" I asked. "Where's he getting off?"

"Oh, he's coming to Wrexham," said Officer Jones. "That's the quickest place to put him on a train back to Cardiff."

My heart sank. There was no way we were going to get Lloyd back in the next twenty minutes before we hit Wrexham. It was a mark of how thoroughly strange my day had been that I was even willing to consider it. Aurelia was screwed, too. Maybe I should get off at the next stop and pretend to have nothing to do with anything. "What's the stop after Chirk?" I asked.

"Ruabon, I think."

"There's a castle at Ruabon, isn't there?" I didn't know anything about Ruabon. I was hoping Officer Jones didn't, either.

"Oh, might be," he said. "Wait, no, you're thinking of Ruthin."

"I could have sworn my guidebook said there was a castle at Ruabon. Or a chapel? Yeah, I think it was a medieval chapel." It was a safe bet that there'd be one or the other. "My ticket's good all day. I bet I could hop off, see it, and catch the next train in an hour."

The train slid to a stop in a puff of pneumatic brakes. The cops on the platform were easy to spot. Aurelia should be flattered that she merited three of them and a patrol car in the parking lot.

I realized my plan to abandon her would never work, for two reasons. First, I was too good a person. Second, she had my phone on her. That was material evidence.

I held my breath, afraid I'd see a curly head disembarking the train in search of her errant dragon, but the only people who got off were the little old lady and a family with a toddler. The doors hissed shut.

As we shuddered back into motion, Officer Jones gave up on the tomato and lowered the bread instead. Lloyd's forked tongue tested the mayonnaise, deemed it acceptable, and proceeded to lick.

As I watched the end of the platform slide past the window, I had an idea. Some answers arrive in a dazzling burst of inspiration, like the answer to the riddle of the fox, the hen, and the sack of corn. The answer to the riddle of the dragon, the magic major and the Welsh transit police arrived as more of a wet *glop.* "I have a stupid dragon question."

"Oh?"

"It's totally immature. But I know my little brother's going to ask when I tell him about this. Do dragons need a litter box?"

His eyebrows rose. I could tell he hadn't thought of that. "I don't know," he said slowly.

Rajesh started to look worried. I imagined that he was thinking of the mop and bucket behind the counter and his pay grade.

"Huh," said Officer Jones. "Rajesh, let's have a cardboard box."

I'd already peeked over the counter to ascertain that the only cardboard boxes present were full of paper plates, paper napkins, and drink cups.

"I can't leave my counter," said Rajesh. "Under the sink in the lavatory, there are boxes for the loo rolls. You could take the loo roles out."

"I can't leave the dragon," said Officer Jones.

"Want me to get one?" I asked brightly. "Watch my tea."

Which was how I escaped the dining car.

Chapter 8: Operation Fflewddur Fflam

"Tuck your hair under your hat," I told Aurelia. We were crammed knee-to-knee in the tiny lavatory in Car 8. "Here, give me your jacket. Outlaws don't wear bright pink."

She elbowed me in the stomach in the process of divesting herself of the jacket. I rolled it up and stuffed it in her backpack. She didn't have another one with her, and I wasn't about to give her my windbreaker, because Officer Jones had already seen me in it. She shivered in her blouse.

"Next time we're trying to decide whose turn it is to unclog the shower drain," I told her, "I want you to remember this."

"You're the best," she agreed.

"I can't believe I'm doing this."

"Seven." She was keeping count of the number of times I'd said that.

When I'd told her my idea, I'd only been half-serious. Anybody with two brain cells to rub together would have abandoned the dragon, aborted the mission, ridden out the media frenzy at her mom's pony farm, and slunk back into Cardiff next week to cough up whatever fine they give out for attempted dragon-napping. I mean, the dragon was arguably hers to start with; once the frenzy died down, it might have all turned out okay. But she had a stubborn streak. She might be about as combative as a lava lamp, but somebody as hapless as Aurelia Ambrose doesn't survive well into her second year in the magic department at Cardiff Uni without a healthy dose of too stupid to quit. I'd dangled a plan. She'd sat up and begged.

"We need a code word," she said as I zipped up her backpack.

"Okay. Shoot."

"Operation Clotted Cream."

"Every time you say that, I'm going to think of operating on a clotted artery."

"Forget it," she said.

"Help me get the toilet paper box out of here."

The cabinet under the sink wasn't locked, but with two of us crammed into the lavatory, there wasn't room to open it all the way. She had to flatten herself against the door and I had to climb up on the lid of the toilet to make room.

"Operation Llanfairpiggledywiggledy," she said.

"I think I've already killed that joke. How about Operation Fflewddur Fflam?" Fflewddur Fflam was the bard character in *Chronicles of Prydain*, and my idea hinged on fast talking and a flare for the dramatic.

"Perfect," she said.

I extracted the toilet paper box. I was going to feel silly carrying a box marked 'C&P Wholesale loo paper' through two passenger cars. I reclaimed my backpack. She kept hers.

"Ready?" I said.

"No. Yes."

"I'd like it noted that I advised against this."

"You advised *for* it, too."

"No, I floated a hypothetical and you decided to take me seriously. Ready?"

"Set. Go."

"Good luck."

"You, too." I opened the lavatory door.

"Marlene?" she whispered after me.

"Yeah?"

"I can't believe you're doing this, either. Thanks."

I shrugged. She pulled the door shut between us. I heard the plastic lock turn.

I walked up the aisle very quickly as the computerized female voice announced, "The next stop is: Wrexham." Timing was important. We hadn't started decelerating yet. I pressed the button and the doors of the dining car slid open.

Officer Jones hadn't moved. Lloyd had mayonnaise on his nose. The bread was clean and dragon-spit shiny.

"Sorry!" I chirped, waving the box. "A bunch of the lavatories were occupied, so I had to walk all the way to the other end of the train, but you won't believe who I saw in Car Fourteen."

Officer Jones sat up suddenly. "You saw her?"

"Well, I dunno, the security footage online is blurry, but this *could* be her. Kind of round face? Curly hair? She's near the luggage rack. She's wearing a white blouse and a sort of salmon-colored jacket and one of those crinkly pleated skirts, if that helps. She's got a purple backpack. I wonder if it's the one she kept the dragon in!"

Officer Jones reached for his phone. Then his hand fell away from it. My brilliant plan hinged on him not being able to resist going to check. It was a big *if.* I wasn't sure if transit cops had the power to make arrests, but I was hoping somebody who was excited to tell a tourist all about Lloyd would be excited enough at least to want to go see for himself.

He looked at Lloyd guiltily.

"Gosh, a real criminal," I burbled. "I'll babysit the dragon if you want! Rajesh can help me."

Rajesh held up his hands in one of those leave-me-out-of-it gestures.

I gave Officer Jones a look that had *Criminal Minds* fangirl written all over it. He looked a little pleased, but also conflicted, so I gave him one more little nudge. "What if she escapes?"

He heaved a big breath and slapped his hands down on his knees. "Well, nothing for it," he said, pushing to his feet.

"I'm sure Lloyd and I will get along just fine." I beamed and took the stool next to the one he'd abandoned. There was still pickle on the soggy sandwich sitting on the counter. I peeled it up and wiggled it for Lloyd. I had his full attention.

"Don't let him out of your sight," said Officer Jones.

"I won't. I promise. Gosh, this is exciting. Can I feature you on my blog?"

"Oh." He looked pleased at the idea. "I suppose. Why not?" And he walked swiftly to the door to give me something to blog about.

"Car fourteen!" I called after him.

Lloyd was definitely interested in the pickle. His head tracked it as we started to decelerate. Outside the window, grubby brick duplexes alternated with corrugated warehouses. I drummed my heels and hoped. My plan hinged on there being another train at the station.

There was. A welcome wall of magenta steel swallowed up the window view. It was a Trans-Cymru commuter, and its doors were open, just like the train schedule had promised. We were golden.

It's hard to make a dramatic entry into a dining car whose automatic door has a two-second delay. I saw Aurelia coming; she swept down the aisle of the passenger car like an avenging Celtic goddess, curls streaming, skirt fluttering. She jabbed the door button with all the momentum of righteous fury. Then she had to wait for two seconds while the door thought about opening.

Rajesh hadn't noticed anything, so I pretended not to, either. I kept the pickle just out of Lloyd's reach. He was getting tired of the game. His tongue flicked sulkily in and out. Clearly, I wasn't as much fun as Officer Jones. His attention was starting to wander, so I dropped the pickle. He pounced.

The door swished open and Aurelia lunged inside. She flashed the crescent symbol—fist closed, pointer finger and pinkie sticking out. In reality, the crescent was a perfectly friendly Wiccan blessing that barely registered on the Emrys scale, but Rajesh didn't know that, and obliged us by yelping and diving behind his counter. I pretended to seize up.

"Leave poor Lloyd alone!" said Aurelia. It was a little less portentous than the "Release my dragon or I'll cast you a heart attack!" that we'd practiced in the lavatory, but it got the same idea across.

Lloyd, trying to get his bottom fangs under the pickle and succeeding only in pushing it around the linoleum, never knew what hit him. The backpack enveloped him.

"Hey," said Rajesh from behind the counter. "Is that the girl from the news?"

The momentum of Aurelia's lightning raid was checked slightly when she discovered the challenges of holding the backpack shut and drawing the zippers at the same time. The backpack thrashed. I couldn't help her. Unconvincingly, Rajesh began to round the counter.

"Stay there or I'll hex you!" she said. He held up his hands, palms out, and retreated. She pointed at me, chanted an arcane-sounding line in Welsh that she may or may not have been reading from the Welsh-language side of the menu above the counter, and snapped her fingers.

She was a better improv artist than I was. It took me a minute to realize I was supposed to unfreeze. Subtle acting was hard to do under the circumstances, but I summoned my best glazed-eyed zombie impression. I knelt—the knee of my jeans made the acquaintance of the pickle—and helped her drag the zippers shut. Lloyd mewled. That was a new sound.

Aurelia surged to her feet and slung the backpack over her shoulder. She ran for the other end of the dining car, jammed the button, and fidgeted in place while the automatic door inched open. Then she was gone.

"What," Rajesh quavered when she was gone, "was that about?"

I zombied out the opposite door.

Chapter 9: I Aid and Abet

Wrexham Central was one of those little two-track stations where both tracks ran between the station and a concrete island. I was on the island. Good news: The Trans-Cymru train was still there, on the other side of our train. Bad news: There was a green metal footbridge crossing the tracks, and in the middle of it, ready to cut Aurelia off at the pass, were two cops.

They don't know for sure who they're looking for, I told myself, which staved off the immediate heart attack; that security footage was blurry, and last time we'd checked, nobody'd come forward and identified her by name. But the police did know what their suspect was wearing, and they were positioned to filter the offloading passengers one by one. I searched desperately for Aurelia and spotted her dithering by a waste bin under the rain canopy, digging through her pockets like she had a wrapper to toss. I managed to catch her eye.

Help, she mouthed.

I can't believe I'm doing this, I mouthed back, and ran ahead of her. I climbed the stairs. From up in the air, I could see across the station to the parking lot. I caught glimpses of flashing blue and yellow lights. The only way the police could possibly have advertised *ambush* more effectively was if they'd turned on the sirens.

I didn't look back to see if Aurelia was behind me. I hoped she knew there was no way I'd get the policemen off the footbridge completely. I might be able to distract them for a few seconds.

There were two of them, a roundish middle-aged man with a name badge that said Davies and a slightly younger woman with her hair scraped back in a claw clip with her name badge covered by an open pocket flap. They both wore bulletproof vests. I hadn't seen many of those in the UK. I wrung my hands and summoned my best anxious-tourist face. "Excuse me? I think someone stole my phone."

The bridge wasn't that wide, and I and my backpack created a pretty effective bottleneck.

"Move aside, please, ma'am," said Officer Davies, flapping his hands. He didn't look nearly as jolly as Officer Jones.

I pressed myself against the rail. "My phone is missing," I insisted. "I had it in Ruabon, I know because I checked my route. I'd do Find My Phone, but there's no Wi-Fi for my laptop. How do I report it stolen?"

A tattooed man squeezed past us, dragging a suitcase that almost swept the legs out from under both cops. I squashed myself closer to the rail.

"There's Wi-Fi in the station," said the woman officer. "You could try in there."

Behind us, my train's brakes hissed.

"That won't help me if my phone is halfway to Chester by the time I get online!" I wailed.

The next person to squeeze past us was a girl with her hair tucked under her rain hat, cradling a purple backpack.

"You're sure it was stolen?" said Officer Davies. "You didn't just drop it?"

"I can check the platform again," I said doubtfully. If I drew this out too much longer, I'd miss the train.

"Go check," he said.

Dammit. I patted my pockets, but they were all clearly flat. I didn't have a phone to miraculously produce. I'd been an idiot to give it to Aurelia. I'd forgotten that what she was missing was her charger, not her phone. Which meant she had a plethora of phones and I had none.

The officers watched me carefully. They probably wanted me out of their way so they could keep watch for their dragon thief. I risked a glance past them and saw Aurelia's curly head bobbing down the last few stairs onto the far platform.

I had the sudden, panicked thought that Officer Jones might be reaching for his walkie-talkie right now to signal to law enforcement that Aurelia had an accomplice. No choice; I did what the officers had told me and headed back the way I'd come. I'd have to duck behind something and "find" my phone. I sent a prayer in the general direction of the Welsh gods that I'd still make it onto the same train as Aurelia.

As I made a show of scanning the ground under the rain shelter, the criminal profile ran through my head. "Our unsub is a Canadian female in her early twenties with appalling acting skills, a pickle print on her jeans, and outsized faith in her own cunning. Likely to be exhibiting signs of nervousness, including the repetition of the phrase 'I can't believe I'm doing this.' Last seen lying through her teeth to an officer of the law. Deport on sight.'"

The scream of a whistle made me jump.

No, I thought. All thoughts of phone cons flew out of my head as I whirled and raced back the way I'd come. *No, no, no, no, no...* Silver medal goes to Canada for the hundred-meter dash. I pounded up the steps, dodging past the last stragglers from the Chester train. I huffed something that might've been "found it" in the direction of Davies and his partner, practically slid down the banister on the other side of the footbridge, and hit the far platform running. I was all prepared to win prizes for the Olympic bar jump through the closing doors, too. But they were already closed.

A nose and two palms pressed the glass on the other side of the doors. The train lurched and lumbered slowly into motion. Its long pink length began to snake past. The reflection swallowed Aurelia long before she probably lost sight of me. As the caboose slid by, I doubled over, hands on knees, panting.

As Aurelia would say—*shite.*

Too late, I thought to look at the schedule board. All I saw was a flicker of motion as the station changed. Now it said Shrewsbury via Many Towns I Can't Pronounce. What'd it said before? *Fricking shite bollocks bloody crapdammit.* I had no idea where Aurelia was going.

"You all right, ma'am?"

I whirled. It was the policewoman. I tried again to see her name tag, but her pocket flap was covering it. She saw me squinting. "I'm Meredith," she said. "What's your name?"

"Marlene."

"Did you find your phone, Marlene?"

I almost said yes, but I was afraid of being caught out. "No," I said. "I couldn't find it, and that was my train that just left. I don't know anything about Wrexham, I couldn't even find it on a map, I'm not even a hundred percent sure which side of the border I'm on, and I have no idea where I'm going."

"Don't panic," said Meredith—I wasn't sure if there was supposed to be an *Officer* in front of that; it could've been a first or a last name—and put a hand on my shoulder. She looked a lot friendlier now that there was no chance of catching a fugitive on her train platform. "Losing your phone's a big deal when you don't know where you are. It'll be all right. Come inside." She steered me into the station. Wrexham's station was a typical brick warming box with benches, a stand with tourist brochures for towns other than Wrexham, which I gathered didn't have a lot to brag about, and a ticket window, currently unmanned. She deposited me on a bench. "I'll find you a missing articles form," she said.

"Thanks," I said, embarrassed. "I'm okay. If there's Wi-Fi here, I can try Find My iPhone." I brightened up when I realized that as long as Aurelia had my phone, I could track her from my laptop. Then I deflated when I remembered my phone was almost dead. I had until its last gasp to get ahold of her, because I could text my own phone from my laptop, but not hers. She wasn't an initiate in the cult of Apple.

"You stay here," said Meredith. "I'll be right back."

While she was gone, I dragged my laptop out of my backpack and opened it. I waited for it to talk to the station Wi-Fi. A train squealed up to a platform and disgorged another bunch of passengers. They trickled through the station. When my laptop finally connected, I pulled up Find My iPhone. My iPhone was, as it turned out, about halfway back to Ruabon. I looked around for Meredith, then quickly pulled up Messages and dashed out a text to myself: "Meet you in Ruabon." I wasn't sure Ruabon was where we wanted to be, but if I took the time to find a more efficient meeting point, my phone might die, and anyway, making things too complicated was likely to end up with Aurelia stranded somewhere even more obscure. I hit send and had to hope she wouldn't be too polite to check my phone. Then I pulled up Google Maps and set about finding a way to get to Ruabon by bus.

When Meredith came back, she had a form with lots of little bureaucratic boxes on it, still warm from the printer. I thanked her, fed her some garbled story about a good Samaritan having found my phone and texted me to say it was in Lost and Found in Ruabon, and ran out the door.

*

I didn't get a great vibe from Wrexham. The area around the train station consisted of strip malls with broken windows. There *was* a chapel, but it looked like it wouldn't be winning any Welsh Heritage grants; the churchyard was full of crumpled Coke bottles and shawarma wrappers. The pavements were covered in cigarette butts. The cloud cover was breaking up, and the light that trickled down had a yellow slant that reminded me it'd be dark in a couple of hours.

The X5 Llangollen stop was supposed to be around the corner from the fire station. There were stops on both sides of the street—my choice of backdrop was the disreputable chapel or a school with plywood over half the windows—and I couldn't tell which stop was mine, because I didn't know which direction Ruabon was from here. My first guess was wrong. I didn't scurry across the street fast enough to flag down the bright purple bus, which rolled right past the empty stop, flashing its "X5 Llangollen" taillight at me. I winged a prayer that it wasn't the last one for the day.

There was nowhere to sit, and the pavement was wet. I shifted from foot to foot, enduring possibly the longest half-hour of my semester. The weight of my backpack made my shoulders ache. I itched to know what the internet was saying about the latest Lloyd sighting. Maybe it would remain one of many. Maybe it'd get drowned out by miraculous visitations across the country. Or maybe the police now knew in exactly which county to put up roadblocks. I kept reaching into my back pocket, ready to look up the news, only to remember all over again that Aurelia had my phone.

The thing about an hour of sustained panic followed by half an hour of standing on your feet at a deserted bus stop on an empty stomach and a few hours of bad couch sleep is that exhaustion has plenty of time to creep up. By the time the next X5 pulled up to the curb, I knew I was in danger of doing something stupid like pillowing my head on my backpack, closing my eyes, and sleeping through my stop.

I had exact change ready, though it took the last of my cash. I took the seat right behind the driver. "Tell me when we get to Ruabon," I said. He grunted.

I pillowed my head on my backpack. I didn't close my eyes. Strip malls with boarded windows petered out, and the long ribbon of country motorway began to wind across a damp landscape sparkling under yellowing sunlight. It's strange how abruptly the twenty-first century can give way. Runny mud crept onto the asphalt, blurring the lane lines. Twisted old apple trees marked the corners of overgrown fields. I watched a flock of magpies leap up from a sunken hollow. When you think of magpies, you think black and white, but Welsh magpies have a dab of blue across the shoulders that flashes like jewels when they fan their wings.

My eyelids felt like weights. I fought to keep them open. In my whimsical mood, I was sure that if I closed them and fell asleep, I'd wake up in the *Mabinogion.*

I wondered how Aurelia and Lloyd were doing. If Aurelia hadn't got my text, we were in trouble. I hoped she'd turn that new manipulative streak of hers to talking somebody out of a charging cord. Or maybe she'd be swallowed up by the *Mabinogion,* too. Maybe we were both headed for a world where charging cords didn't matter.

I swear I only closed my eyes for a second. There wasn't even time for a whole anxiety dream, just the opening credits of one of those where's-my-exam-room classics. My archaeology exam was taking place at the top of a train station clock tower and the entrance was beneath one of a dozen underpasses, and there were magpies flitting around my head cheeping at me about how easy it would be to just fly up to the window and how only an idiot couldn't manage an underpass transfer. I woke up with amber sunlight slanting sideways through the bus windows.

"Last stop!" called the driver.

Chapter 10: I Do What I Told Aurelia Not To

The driver ejected me with a cheery wave. "Enjoy your stay!" he called. I was still fuddled from the magpie dream as the doors shut behind me, and for a critical moment I couldn't summon the name of the town I was supposed to be in to ask if this was it. The bus pulled out and disappeared.

Something was wrong. As my dream-panic trickled away, it made way for a new kind. Panic comes in many flavors. This was the slow-onset panic that socks you in two stages. The first is when you begin to suspect you've screwed up. The second can't really get up a full head of steam till you've had time to plumb the full depths of your incompetence and enumerate the consequences. I had a creeping suspicion I wasn't in Ruabon.

The bus had left me under a wrought-iron lamppost on a two-lane stone bridge. On the other side of the rail, a wide, slow, shallow, dark river dimpled over submerged rocks. It was placid except for a jagged whitewater scar where it ripped across some underwater obstacle. A few hardy bushes clung to flat rocks in mid-current.

Boxy stone buildings overhung the far bank. Their balconies dangled precariously over the current. Further upstream, screened by bare branches, I saw a spire with a slate roof, and beneath it, the stained-glass windows of a sandstone chapel. Beyond, the wall of a valley rose steeply, banded with dark stands of evergreen. The sun had already slipped behind it, leaving the bottom of the river valley draped in premature evening murk.

A solitary car rolled across the bridge, its headlights stretching my shadow across the pavement. They washed across a black sign with white letters spelling out DEE SIDE CAFE. I took a deep breath and supposed that made this the Dee River.

I still had no idea where the Dee River was, and I had no phone, and I was running low on cash and daylight. I turned, hoping for a road sign or a cafe with Wi-Fi—anything that'd help me come up with a plan. Right away my eyes lit on a blessed sight: a raised footbridge, this one with yellow half-timbered sides and a shingled roof. Beneath it, train tracks. There was a stone platform with a station sign. It was facing the wrong way, so I couldn't tell what it said. I hoisted my backpack and started walking.

There was a damp evening nip in the air. The valley smelled like soil and wet stone. It was quiet. Every minute or two, a car rolled by, its tires crunching on the pavement, but in between, the only sounds were wind soughing through leaves and water parting around the sharp pediments of the medieval bridge. A crow rasped. I balled my hands in my pockets. The pads of my fingers felt cold against my palms.

The train station was too quiet. I knew before I got there that I'd find the gate closed. It wasn't a modern ticket-scanning gate, but a wrought-iron affair with clubbed spikes at the top, girdled by a chain and padlock. Above the door, carved into a granite lintel, were the words LLANGOLLEN HISTORIC RAILWAY.

Dammit, I mouthed at the grate, and then stood there several minutes longer with no idea what to do next. Finally, for lack of a better idea, I began to walk back toward the bridge. It was amazing how quickly the darkness pooled now that the sun had sunk below the ring of hills. Another car rolled past, its headlights washing the road in two distinct arcs. Where they raked a glass storefront on the corner, many sets of tiny eyes sparked suddenly at me and vanished again. I nearly jumped out of my windbreaker. *Llangollen Taxidermy,* said the sign on the window, and on the other side of the glass were small, mangy bodies, stiff with age. A magpie with glass eyes and a gap in its tailfeathers perched on a log. I took a shaky breath and thought, *there's a bit of local color.*

I stationed myself across the street from the bus stop and proceeded to waffle there while the evening congealed and my stomach got emptier and no bus came. If I walked away, I was bound to do it just in time to watch the bus roll through. If I stayed where I was, the bus might never come. The one that had dropped me off could easily have been the last for the evening.

I lingered a long time on the bridge. A damp breeze was stirring over the water. I turtled my neck deep in my windbreaker and wished I'd packed for a cross-country quest rather than a lecture.

Bats or night birds cheeped overhead, not much more than specks of fluttering movement against the sky. I was struck all over again by the contrast between Llangollen and Wrexham. Here, I thought, there'd be no jumping aboard a train and being two towns over in fifteen minutes. If I wanted out of here, I was going to have to do it the old-fashioned way, on my own feet and without a phone.

I didn't know how.

Indecision kept me there long after I'd given up hoping for a bus. It was the cold that finally forced me to start walking. Most of the town looked like it was on the Dee Side Cafe bank, so that was the direction I picked.

Past the cafe, a wide street stretched away up a very gentle slope. Flower baskets hung beneath the lampposts, spilling over with out-of-season purple and white and pink begonias and trailing green vines. Warm light spilled through the windows of close-packed shops and bed-and-breakfasts. The street had a Victorian look, owing to decorative turrets and old-fashioned mullions that broke the light into diamond patterns on the pavement. The place was very green, and a lot of the buildings were gray stone, which gave me the funny idea that it had all grown out of the soil.

My teeth chattered, and my insides were that special combination of cold and hungry that results in a shiver that turns into an ache that wrings you out. I fantasized about a crackling fireplace and a hot lamb stew. I knew I didn't have the time or money to stop. I had to find my way back to Aurelia. Funny; I'd been worried about *her* getting stranded. I was realizing I'd been showing off a little when I told her she could always pop into a coffeeshop and find a hostel. I mean, theoretically that was true, but my definition of short notice was twenty-four hours, not *one* hour, and I couldn't afford a bed and breakfast and there was no guarantee there'd be a hostel I could get to on foot now that the buses weren't running.

It was that time of evening when daytime shops and cafes are starting to turn over their signs and lock up but their employees haven't accumulated on the patios of the pubs yet. It was quiet enough that I could still hear the river.

A blue sign nailed to the side of a sweet shop told me I was on Castle Street. Arbitrarily, I turned right. I wasn't sure what I was looking for. I was just drifting. Somehow, I didn't think I'd find a Caffe Nero here.

The side street was quieter. A jumble of lofts and mews tangled the corner so that even though the pavement was straight, it all looked organic. A place you could get lost in. I was just starting to think about turning around and throwing myself on the mercy of one of the pubs when I saw warm light spilling through a doorway up ahead.

It wasn't the light that caught my eye. It wasn't the doorway it spilled from, either, although that belonged to a two-story beige-brick decagon punctuated with windows the shape of upside-down gonfalons. A neat little parking lot bracketed the odd building, separating it from its cuboid neighbors and making it look like a can of beans on a plate.

What snagged my attention was the bowl on the rim of the stone planter near the door. The bowl was ceramic and full of milk. It was enough to turn my feet. There was a small sign over the door that was hard to read in the fading light, but to the left, above one of the windows, was a bigger plasticized posterboard that said *Amgueddfa*—anybody's guess what that meant— *Llangollen Museum of Local History.*

The door was standing open. I stuck my head inside. The museum was a single rotunda with a gallery ringing the second story. It looked like a classroom; there were a few glass cases, but most of the displays were posterboards on easels. To one side of the door was a bulletin board stuck full of printout flyers for "Storytelling Night" and "Bran's Castle Excursion" and a call for extras in a Welsh-language short film. A papier-mâché Cistercian monk guarded an alcove. There was a case full of arrowheads and a standing runestone. When I leaned over the poster behind the stone, I saw a misplaced apostrophe on the third line. My first thought was that the archaeology here was homebrewed. My second was Aurelia's "story-truths," which reminded me of Aurelia, which reminded me why I'd come in. I looked around. "Hello?"

No answer except for a whine from the direction of a desk near the wall. The desk appeared to be both admissions booth and gift shop; an empty spinny chair was flanked by a rack of bracelets and a cash register, plus a further jumble of flyers in plastic stands. I looked for anything resembling a Wi-Fi password.

"Don't suppose *you* know the password," I said to the source of the whine, which was a funny-looking whitish greyhound in a corduroy bed behind the desk. Its ears were russet. It watched me through half-closed colorless eyes.

At least that meant there had to be an owner somewhere nearby. I didn't see anyone, and outside the windows, the sky was getting rapidly darker. If there was no Wi-Fi here, I should keep moving, but it was warm, and *ye Welsh gods* was I tired of making decisions today. The corners of my eyes pricked. I was going to feel really stupid if I started crying.

"Hello," said a voice behind me. I jumped and spun around.

Something about Llangollen had put me in a whimsical frame of mind, because my first thought was that the woman's long hair was white as moonbeams, and my second was that she'd materialized so silently. I felt a flash of absurd guilt, like I'd been caught trespassing. I opened my mouth to explain.

"You're a bit late, dear," she said, preempting me. "I'm just closing up." She had a lovely accent, somehow different from the local ones. I couldn't place it.

"That's okay," I said. "Sorry. It's just, I'm lost, and I think I'm marooned here, and my friend and my phone are gods-only-know-where, and I can't find Wi-Fi—" My voice hitched. I veered rapidly onto safer ground. "Is the milk outside for the Fair Family?"

The curator smiled. "Everyone always assumes it's for a cat."

"My roommate leaves milk and honey on her windowsill, too." Aurelia was always hoping we'd get fairies. Mostly what we got was wasps, but hope springs eternal. "That's what made me come in here," I plunged on. "I figured, well—" What I'd unconsciously figured was that somebody who left out milk for the Fair Family might be sympathetic to Aurelia, which I realized now was wholly irrelevant because I was the one who needed help, "—I hoped your museum might have Wi-Fi. I need to get ahold of my roommate. We got separated, and the only phone I can contact from my laptop is mine, which is with her, but it's on its last legs, and if it dies before I can tell her to wait for me in Ruabon, I'll never find her. Not that I can get to Ruabon, either." I didn't quite say *I'm stranded,* because that tends to worry people.

"Don't cry," she said.

"I'm not," I said, embarrassed, and dissolved completely. I blame the adrenaline crash. I scrubbed my eyes on the cuff of my windbreaker. "Sorry," I said.

"Don't be. Do you know your friend's number?"

"No. Wait. Yes. It must be in my contacts." I set down my backpack gratefully on the carpet and unzipped it.

"I'll be right back," she said. "Take a seat."

Thoroughly humiliated, I took her spinny chair. The dog looked at me with fathomless eyes. Having had enough of animals today, I ignored it. I opened my laptop and found Aurelia's number. I waited. My foot jiggled.

The curator was back a few minutes later with a pink mug that said *Cwtch* with a picture of two sheep hugging. "Your teeth are chattering," she said by way of explanation, pushing it across the desk to me. It was full of steaming tea.

"Thank you. Sorry. Thanks." I wrapped my hands around it, feeling foolish. "Sorry," I added again.

"Don't apologize." From nowhere, she produced a phone. It looked incongruous in her hands. She passed it to me. It was one of those giant off-brand ones with enormous graphics. A crack ran from one corner to the home button like forked lightning, but the screen was spotless—my fingers, as I punched in Aurelia's number, left unsightly prints, and I wondered how the curator had managed not to.

I held my breath as the line rang. I was terrified that all I'd get was Aurelia's perky voice recording.

There was a *click*. "Marlene?"

"Aurelia. Thank goodness. Where are—"

She was trying to ask me the same question at the same time. Our words collided and jumbled, and we both broke off.

"Sorry, sorry, sorry," she said. "You first. Where are you?"

"Llangollen."

"Where?"

"Exactly. Where are *you*?"

"Ty Mawr Country Park."

"Where's that?"

"Wrexham. I tried to come back for you. But there's a guard outside the train station, and the buses aren't running anymore. And it's getting cold. Lloyd doesn't look so good."

The curator was kneeling by the corduroy bed, communing with the dog. I hoped she wasn't listening. "I don't suppose you can walk the Red Scare into a pet-friendly pub to warm up."

"No. I've bundled him in my jacket, and I've got my arms wrapped around him too, but there's nowhere for us to go."

"I think you're going to have to call your mom."

A long hesitation. "...Yeah. I was hoping to preface it with *Hi, Mom, surprise! Here I am, and here's a bag of your favorite Welsh cakes from that stall you like in Cardiff.*"

"Hey, it's better than camping out in a park overnight. I think you better call her before your phone dies."

"What are *you* going to do?"

Keys jingled, a reminder that the curator was closing up and I was going to end up out in the cold again soon. "I'm going to improvise." I didn't want to know what my bank account would look like by the end of the weekend. "Call your mom. That's what moms are for. You'll be fine. Well, once she finishes throttling you."

"You, too. Be fine, I mean, not be throttled." She still sounded dubious. I had to have faith that her fear of being stranded in a park with a hypothermic dragon overnight would outweigh her fear of her mom.

"Course I will," I said. "Good luck with the quest. You don't need a sidekick."

"Thanks. I'll be okay. I think." *Click.*

I pulled the phone away from my ear, feeling oddly let down. Which was weird, because I hadn't meant to come along on Aurelia's stupid quest in the first place.

"All sorted?" said the curator in the tone of somebody who was prepared to brew more tea if it wasn't.

"Yes," I said. "Thank you. She's at Ty Mawr Country Park. She's got a ride. She's got things more in hand than I do." I handed the phone back.

She pocketed it and shouldered her bag. "Are you coming?"

"Where?"

"Ty Mawr, of course. It's fifteen minutes from here. And *somebody* has been behind a desk all day and needs a walk."

I blinked. Several possible responses occurred to me—relief, humiliation, dismay, bemusement. My mouth, which thought faster than my brain, said, "Can I fill my water bottle with hot water first?"

Chapter 11: The Guardian

"Your roommate sounds like someone I'd get on with,"
said the curator as her old sedan rattled up the side of
the valley. Being crammed into the front seat of a small
car with her, my feet rolling on old takeout baggies,
should've broken her spell, if the sheep mug hadn't been
enough to convince me that she was human. But there
was something about her. It wasn't frightening. She
just...I don't know. *Touched the world lightly*, was the
slightly giddy thought I'd had as we'd crossed the bridge.
Her car should've smelled like dog and takeout, but it
didn't smell like anything at all.

"My roommate would love your museum," I said
politely. "She loves stories."

"And what about you?"

"I'm an archaeology major," I said. "I guess I like
things I can hold in my hand."

The headlights traveled across the trunks of the slim
pines and gleamed on the leaves of waxy bushes. Beyond
their white circle, there was nothing but night. There
weren't many streetlights up here at the edge of the
Clwydian Range.

"There's quite a lot of archaeology around here," she
said.

"Castle Dinas Bran?" I'd seen a poster to that effect in the museum. And, bowing to the temptation to show off what I'd learned a quarter of an hour ago, I added, "Seat of the Princes of Powys?"

She scoffed. "Newcomers. We have Roman gravestones, Celtic crosses, and a chain of hillforts on the peaks of every hill in the Clwydian Range between here and the ocean. You just have to know where to look."

The road wound along the top of a ridge. To our left, the ground dropped away. Beyond the guardrail could've been the edge of Annwn, the Otherworld. Then, with jarring suddenness, we rounded a bend and confronted a pair of glowing red eyes. It took several seconds for them to resolve themselves into the taillights of a Peugeot idling on the road ahead of us. Beyond was a white plastic barrier.

"Hmph," said the curator. She didn't sound surprised; only faintly irked.

A flagger was holding up our lane while a pair of policemen searched a car on the other side of the barrier. They were dishearteningly thorough. I watched them open the doors and fold down the seats. They made the owner pop the boot. They shone their flashlights into the glove compartment.

Anxiously, I said, "They couldn't possibly block every road out of Wrexham, right?"

"Oh, if they pinch off the A5152 ring, they'd have the town pretty well bottled," said the curator. "But they won't."

"Really?"

"If they're looking for what I think they're looking for," she said, "they'll block off every road in Clwyd and half of Denbighshire."

The police finished searching the car on the other side of the barrier. The flagger let it through. They rounded the barrier and started on the Peugeot. I wondered how on earth Aurelia's mom was going to get to us, much less how we were all going to get out.

The police let the Peugeot go. As they approached the curator's door, she rolled down the window. "Good evening, officer. What's this about?"

The officer leaned down. He was careful not to shine the flashlight in our eyes. "Have you ladies seen a small red dragon lately?"

It was probably my imagination that his partner was looking right at me. In my best vapid tourist voice, I said, "Oh, I've been *reading* about that."

"Disgraceful," said the curator, with feeling. "All this fuss, and for what? For a poor creature who shouldn't have been locked up in the first place."

I blinked.

"Would you mind popping the boot for us?" his partner said.

She popped the boot. They carried out their inspection, then waved us on. The flagger let us past the barrier. As the curator rolled up her window, she said, "How the little fellow would have got to Wrexham, of all places, I don't know. Last I checked, he was in St. Fagan's, or was it Hay-on-Wye?"

"It's like Elvis sightings."

She laughed. "Best of luck to him."

We hit two more barriers on our way to Ty Mawr Country Park. Finally the car turned onto a gravel lane and then a small car park. Grass rolled away in all directions, dotted with stands of bushy alder. A winding line of bare trees somewhere ahead of us marked the edge of the river. The curator parked the car. "Here we are," she said. "The aqueduct is that way." She pointed upriver.

It'd gotten chilly, that special spring-night kind that washed us in damp clammy air as we opened the car doors. "Now," she said as she circled around to the boot, "where's your friend?"

"I'd hate to drag you all over the park in this cold," I hedged, imagining the dog and the dragon coming face-to-face. "I'll find her. Thank you so, so much for the ride. I never would have got here without you."

She opened the boot. The greyhound eeled out so smoothly his claws didn't even click. He was flesh and blood—I'd checked by scratching his ears—but in the chilly night, he could've been trotting just the other side of the veil between worlds. At the edge of the car park was one of those black and white signs, *Please keep dogs leashed.* It would never even have occurred to me to apply it to him.

"We need a stretch of the legs," the curator announced. "And I'm not leaving a young woman alone in the dark in Wrexham. Lead on."

I hesitated, but I had no real way to get rid of her. As we set off down the trail, I had to hope Lloyd would be in the backpack.

Sometimes, between the trees, I could see a glimmer of orange that probably sat at the top of a pole and came from an electric generator, but the lattice of branches made it flicker like distant torchlight. Paths and trails crisscrossed our side of the river. To our left, a great black hulk loomed above the bank, its arches lit from beneath, like a medieval bridge on a massive scale, or a Roman aqueduct. It was the only landmark.

"Can I borrow your phone again?" I asked, suspecting we could wander around here all night and never find Aurelia.

The curator handed it over, but when I redialed Aurelia, there was no answer. Her phone must have finally given up the ghost. I tried my phone, too, but it'd probably died before hers.

In the end, it wasn't us that found her. The greyhound's nose turned like a compass needle, and silently it shot away across the grass.

"Oh!" I said.

The curator was unperturbed. "So that's where they are," she said.

I'd never told her there was a *they.* I'd only mentioned Aurelia.

Mud sucked at the soles of my shoes and my heart climbed my throat as I followed her. We found the dog and dragon sniffing each other's butts in the shelter of a little copse of trees as Aurelia tried to interpose her foot between them. She was chanting "Cut that out, stop that! Quit it, leave off" while conspicuously not using Lloyd's name. When she caught sight of us, she trailed off. The greyhound's tail was wagging. Lloyd's was drooping. So was his neck. He did look cold.

I whirled on the curator. I opened my mouth, not sure what excuse was going to come out of it. What came out was air as Aurelia collided with me. She threw her arms around me. "Marlene!" she said. "I thought I'd lost you!"

"No, you lost yourself. I'm right here." I gave her a quick squeeze so she'd release me. "It's okay. Hang on, we've got something to sort out."

Aurelia went wide-eyed as she realized that Lloyd was prancing about right under the curator's nose. Well, not prancing. Trudging squelchily. I scrambled for an explanation. But the curator wasn't paying attention to Lloyd at all. She was smiling at us. "I'm glad you two found each other," she said.

"Thanks," I said uncertainly.

"Do you have a plan?"

"No," said Aurelia, just as warily.

"Yes," I said at the same time. "Her mom will pick us up. It's okay, it's all sorted out."

"No, she won't," said Aurelia. "She says there are roadblocks. She saw something about them on the news. She went to look up where they were. And then my phone died. So I'm not sure where we are on that."

The greyhound trotted over to the curator, tail wagging. The curator bent down and picked up a stick. She waved it under his nose. Then she reached out to wave it under Lloyd's, too. She drew back her arm and hurled it. The greyhound raced after it. Lloyd, after a moment's slow consideration, turned around and limped in the same general direction.

"You can borrow my phone," the curator said.

"Can I?" said Aurelia. "That'd be wonderful. Thank you, thank you. Maybe we can walk to meet my mom somewhere. You know, so she doesn't have to wait at, like, six different roadblocks. Are the police stopping pedestrians?"

"They might stop pedestrians taking a dragon for a walk," said the curator. "Though I'm sure it'd all be sorted out once they saw that he was brown."

"Brown?" Aurelia echoed.

I could have kicked her.

The greyhound trotted back with the stick and dropped it at the curator's feet. She produced a doggie biscuit. Lloyd limped back into the copse, wheezing. Another biscuit appeared. In a long-suffering sort of way, he brought out sit-up-and-beg. She leaned down to inspect him. In the tone of someone choosing a paint color for her wall, she said, "Brown, I think. He looks brown to me." She drew back her arm and threw the stick. The greyhound pelted after it. "Though I wouldn't parade him too openly," she added. "All dragons are the same color in the dark, and everyone is terribly wound up. Now, call your mum."

Obediently, Aurelia began to dial. The curator turned to me. "By the way, Marlene, I forgot to mention one other interesting bit of local archaeology. Have you ever heard of Offa's Dyke?"

Offa's Dyke was an earthen embankment that ran nearly the entire length of the Welsh border. Whether or not the Saxon king Offa built it was a subject for debate, but clearly it was hostile; it went out of its own way to provide a clear view into Wales. "What about it?" I asked.

"There's a trail," said the curator. "It runs along the top of the dyke, or alongside it, almost the entire length of the Clwydian Range. Very popular with hikers and backpackers in the summer. I think you'd like it—if you've got good hiking boots and a lot of energy, it'll feed you a diet of two hill forts a day."

I started to catch on. "It's a nature path?"

"So far from the road, you can't even hear the traffic."

I kicked Aurelia in the ankle and mouthed, "Offa's Dyke."

Her eyes widened. Then she said, "Mam? Hi! It's me. I borrowed a phone."

Carefully, I said to the curator, "If I did a day trip out here to hike part of Offa's Dyke, and I wanted to *end* in Wrexham—you know, to catch the train back to Cardiff in the evening—where would I start?"

She was watching her greyhound trot back with the stick, so I couldn't see her eyes, but the twinkle was in her voice. "Oh, Moel Fenlli, I should say. There's a lovely hill fort. One of the highest peaks in the Clwydian Range, you know. You can see for miles. And it's the middle of nowhere—like you never left sub-Roman Britain."

Aurelia was watching us from the corner of her eye. "What?" she said into the phone. "Really, they go that far? Okay, try, um, Moel Fenlli. Is *that* outside the cordon?" There was a long pause, in which Lloyd staggered back into the copse, wheezing, and the curator wrestled the stick away from the greyhound and flung it again. Lloyd watched wearily as it sailed over his head. The greyhound nearly trampled him. He watched it go, looking like he was weighing his pride against his frigid metabolism and the possibility of more biscuits.

"Good!" Aurelia said. "Hang on, can you look up directions? I'll write them down, and Marlene is, like, a navigation genius; we'll figure it out. Ready? Okay, start."

Lloyd lay down on the curator's shoes.

"You're going to have to thaw the poor fellow sooner or later," she said.

"I know. He'll be okay once we get him in the backpack with my water bottle."

"So *that's* what the hot water was for."

Aurelia finished negotiations with her mom. She'd pulled out a notebook. How she could see what she was writing, I wasn't sure, nor how we were going to see what she had written without a phone flashlight between us. I hoped she had a spell for that.

"Love you anyway, too, Mam," she said dutifully, and hung up.

The greyhound brought the stick back and dropped it at the curator's feet.

"You know," the curator said, "it's rather cold. If you girls are settled, I think we'll be off. Marlene, it was lovely to meet you. And Aurelia, you're welcome at the Llangollen Museum anytime." She didn't whistle to the greyhound—she didn't have to. It was just there at her heels as she turned to go. Over her shoulder, she added, "Aurelia, if you're going to leave milk and honey for the Fair Family, light a candle. They're creatures of summer; they'll come to warmth."

There was a tug at my ankle. I had to bend over to detach Lloyd's claw from my shoelace. I swear I only looked away for five seconds, but when I looked up, the curator and her greyhound were just gone. I hadn't heard retreating footsteps. Like fog or a fairy ring, they'd evaporated into the clear night.

Chapter 12: The Castle of Gwydion

In daylight, the hike from Ty Mawr to Moel Fenlli would take a good hiker in decent boots six hours. I know because I looked it up later. We were bad hikers in, respectively, wet sneakers and kitten heels. One of us was carrying a slowly thawing dragon. That, if you were wondering, was me. Aurelia was trying to conjure a wisp in a plastic baggie she'd found in a garbage can. Yes, wisp as in will-o'-the.

"It'd be easier if I had my thaumaturgical biochemistry notes," she panted as we slogged uphill. It was miles to the dyke; we were following paved roads for the most part, but any flicker of blue and red lights sent us clambering over garden fences to go around the barriers.

"Isn't thaumabiochem the exam you had to re-sit?" I asked.

"Well...sort of," said Aurelia. "But I did okay on the wisp bit. It's not that hard; you just need swamp conditions, a bioluminescent agent, a thaumaturgical catalyst, and a sacrifice. Wisps are predatory." Her swamp conditions were a handful of mud and grass in the bottom of the baggie. Her sacrifice was a snail we'd found in the middle of the road that was going to get itself run over by a car anyway, so we were doing the species a favor by taking it out of the gene pool. I wasn't convinced that there'd be a wisp in the bag by the time we left the streetlights behind, so when we passed a Spar that looked like it was still open, I planted Aurelia and Lloyd on a bench out of sight, then ducked inside. Two orange sodas, a bottled espresso macchiato, three hot dogs, and a glowstick later, I retrieved them. "I figured everyone's blood sugar could do with a boost," I said as we kept walking. One of the hot dogs went into the backpack, sans bun.

My heels hurt before we'd even left the suburbs. As the ground rose, the lights of Wrexham bunched together below us like they were gathering up to spring. Around us, the hills spread out like a black blanket. "It's easy to see how travelers rode their horses right off cliffs in the olden days," I mused. "You don't realize how dark it is when you leave the city lights behind."

"You haven't seen real darkness yet," she promised. "Wait till we get into the hills."

"Been lost at night in the hills before?"

"Just grew up in the country."

When the hot dogs were gone, I passed her one of the sodas. "We'll do caffeine next," I promised. "I figure we should split the macchiato. Where we're going, the loo paper grows on bushes and the loos *are* bushes, so, you know, take it slow on the liquids."

Lloyd got heavier as time went on. I felt like we'd walked miles already, but every time I turned around, the town lights were still on our heels. "I feel like Wrexham is following us," I said.

"Now I have a funny image in my head," said Aurelia. "The twenty-first century as a stain of orange lights, creeping after us as we try to escape it. Like a big electric amoeba."

"Electric amoeba?"

"Sorry. I'm so tired. Give me the caffeine."

It could've been worse. It could've been raining.

Our path climbed slowly. It had been paved when it left Ty Mawr, but by the time we hit the first kissing gate, the concrete had given way. The only good thing about climbing uphill was that water ran down instead of pooling. Rather than mud, the path was just slightly squelchy gravel-studded dirt. I cracked the glowstick and we held it to the page of Aurelia's spiral-bound notebook.

"Oops," she said as we held it close to the page. She'd faithfully written all the steps her mom had relayed to her. All on the same line.

"It's like a portrait of that thing you exorcised from the shower drain that one time," I said.

"I think I remember where we're going."

"If we fall off a cliff, my last words will be 'are you sure about that?'"

"It's straight-ish," she said. "There are three kissing gates between us and the first hill fort. You'll recognize a hill fort when you see it, right? You're an archaeologist; of course you will. Offa's Dyke Path runs below it, and once we find *that,* we just follow it sort of north."

"Which way's north?"

"I don't know! Isn't there a star for that?"

We walked.

*

One gate had a sign hanging on it that said "Bull in field." We decided detouring wasn't a good idea, because if we got turned around, we might never find the track again. Fortunately, we never saw the bull. More importantly, the bull never saw us.

*

We took a potty break in a copse of bare trees. We tried to convince Lloyd to come out of the backpack long enough to go, but he wouldn't uncoil from the water bottle. I told him if he peed on me, I'd stake him out for the bull.

*

Aurelia's wisp never did materialize. We didn't really need it, because the glowstick was still working, but it was the spirit of the thing. "They're native to Denbighshire, so that's not the problem," she said. "Maybe it wants a better sacrifice."

"*I* sure wouldn't jump into a baggie for a roadkill snail," I said.

"You're right. Help me find a better bug."

Which is how I got to run up and down a farmer's fence for seven minutes till I found a smallish beetle to put in the baggie. Then she tried to make me carry the baggie.

*

I didn't know stars came in that color. It was like once we lost the Wrexham amoeba for good, the sky turned its brightness up to 100%. You could see the Milky Way.

"What's 'Milky Way' in Welsh?" I asked.

"Caer Wydion," she said. "The Castle of Gwydion."

"Why?"

"I don't think anyone knows."

*

We reached Offa's Dyke. It was a low wave in the turf, like a breaker just before it breaks. I clambered down over the Walesward edge to satisfy myself that it was an earthwork. Starlight turned the trail ahead of us into a pale line across the tops of the bracken-roughened slopes, like a trickle of milk. A milky way on the ground, and Gwydion's hill fort in the sky.

"Caffeine," I said, holding out my hand. Aurelia passed me the macchiato.

*

I was walking on the backs of my sneakers by the time we crested the first hill. Up here, nothing grew higher than our ankles, as if the wind had sheared it off. Coarse dark patches of heather swallowed the moonlight.

The night smelled like mud. It was a clean smell. That's not an oxymoron. Dirty is gasoline and pavement. Up here, we were keeping company with mud and heather and ancient half-erased earthworks, and it was all quiet except for the soft crunch of the gravel under our shoes.

I couldn't tell how high we were, because there were hardly any lights on the floor of the valley. The whole world shrank to the size of me and Aurelia and Lloyd sandwiched between heather and stars.

*

I was still thinking about Caer Gwydion as the dyke trail sank into a divot between the hills. "It's like footprints left by a story," I said.

"Huh?"

"Gwydion and the Milky Way. It's like, there must have *been* a story, at one point, explaining why the Milky Way is Gwydion's castle. And that story went walking across other stories, leaving footprints. And then it evaporated, because it was an oral story, and so many oral stories are never written down. But some of the stories it walked across, *those* were written down, and so we have the name 'Caer Gwydion,' but not the story about Gwydion building a castle in the stars."

Wordlessly, Aurelia held out the dregs of the macchiato.

"Have you read *Culhwch and Olwen?*" I asked, ignoring it.

"No."

I threw up my hands. "It's *your* cultural heritage. Why have I read more of your mythology than you have?"

"Because it's exotic to you."

"Fair point."

A copse of hawthorns flanked the trail. They rattled bare branches like skeletal fingers over our heads. Something hooted. I wasn't sure if it was an owl or a pigeon. It was very dark in the divot, and the crunch of the gravel took on a wet lisp, like the water had run downhill and pooled there.

"Culhwch and Olwen," Aurelia prompted.

"Oh. Right. I remember. It's in the *Mabinogion,* and at one point it infodumps this long list of names. Not even names of characters who show up again in Culhwch's story, just a list of people in King Arthur's court. There's a messenger who can run across the tops of the trees. And there's one warrior who, anything he carries in his arms, no one can see it. Or Cei, like Sir Kay from Arthurian legend—there's this bit that goes something like, 'Cei had this peculiarity, that he could exist nine nights without sleep. A wound from his sword, no physician could stitch. When it pleased him, he could render himself as tall as the highest tree. So great was the heat of his nature that when his companions were cold, he was as a dry hearth to them.' Dr. Pine, my mythology prof, she said, he's so hot he evaporates the rain, he changes size, he inflicts injuries that don't heal, he doesn't sleep, doesn't that sound like fire? Like maybe Cei was originally a fire spirit, and he sort of got Christianized into Sir Kay the knight, and we'll never really know very much about that fire spirit. Just the footprints that he left in that list of names in *Culhwch and Olwen.*" I blinked. "I'm sure I was going somewhere with all this."

"Okay," said Aurelia. "Maybe caffeine *isn't* what you need."

I was quiet all the way up the next slope. I swear Lloyd gained fifteen pounds on the uphills. At least he wasn't fidgeting.

We'd probably been walking for two hours by then, though it was hard to tell without a clock between us. The soles of my feet ached from walking on the folded-down backs of my sneakers, which I was doing because my heels hurt worse. I was going to have blisters in some interesting places tomorrow. But I was a hiker; I'd live. By the time we neared the top of the second hill, I was starting to see the problem with our plan, which was that

Aurelia lived a sedentary life, and also, she was in kitten heels.

"Need a rest?" I asked.

"I'm okay," she said unconvincingly. "I'm not the one carrying the dragon."

"Yeah, but we still have ages to go. Let's get to the top of the hill and sit down."

We stepped off the trail and clambered up a steep turf embankment. It crested and dipped into a trough about waist-deep, then rose again, just taller than we were. The trough wound away in both directions, encircling the top of the hill. It was muddy at the bottom.

"Aurie?" I said.

"Yes?" She was bent over with hands on knees, panting.

"How many kissing gates have we climbed over?"

"Um...two? Three?"

"It better have been three."

"Why?"

"Meet your first hill fort."

She ran her hands through the grass. "Oh. Are you sure? It just looks like a bump in the ground."

"Pretty sure. Stay here." I plopped Lloyd down next to her, then took the glow stick and climbed the far side of the trough. The turf dipped and rose again. From the air, a hill fort looks like what you get when you draw several concentric rings in dry sand, except on a massive scale. From the ground, it's a little harder to tell, but on the far side of the last embankment, the top of the hill leveled out, and I almost tripped on a small cairn. The cairn probably had more to do with modern hikers than ancient villagers, but it was a good hint that we were sitting on something that other people had stopped to see, too.

I paused there for a moment. There's not a lot to look at in a hill fort, but seeing wasn't the point. It was enough to know that I was standing in the same place a girl like me stood two thousand years ago. I don't believe in ghosts, but some places just have *echoes.* The wind carries snatches of an extinct language, and if you look over your shoulder, the flap of motion might have been bobbing heather, but might also have been a footfall. For a few minutes, it was just me and the ramparts. The back of my neck prickled. Funny how it's perfectly possible to be afraid of something you don't believe in. I got up and went back the way I'd come, walking slowly.

Aurelia was where I'd left her. She sat barefoot and cross-legged in the grass, flexing her toes. She'd peeled off her boots and socks. I dropped into the grass next to her and stuck the glow stick upright in her boot. "Yep," I said. "It's a hill fort. You all right?"

"I'll live."

We were both quiet for a couple of minutes. I lay back to stare up at all the stars in Gwydion's castle.

"I wonder how many branches there were," she said abruptly.

"What?"

"The Four Branches of the Mabinogi. Why four? Three's the important number in Welsh myth. So if there was going to be a set of core myths, or whatever, you'd have three. Four is kind of random. So why stop there?

Maybe there was a fifth, and we just don't have it, and we don't even know how to recognize its footprints."

"That's why you need to invent a time travel spell."

"Or maybe we're still writing them." There was a whimsical quaver in her voice. "Maybe *we're* the fifth branch."

I pushed myself up on one elbow. "That's a thought."

"Well, we're always making new stories, aren't we? Ours will disappear too, and in two thousand years, two more uni girls will lie on the grass in the foundations of the Percival building and wonder who were Marlene, who could carry a dragon on her back and find a hill fort on a dark mountain without a map, and Aurelia Ambrose, who had a beetle in a baggie, and what their story was."

"No, they won't."

"Why not?"

"Because the internet is forever."

She rubbed her eyes. "Good point." She patted the grass till her hand closed on a sock. "We should probably keep moving."

*

From Wrexham to Moel Fenlli on Offa's Dyke is a journey through Denbighshire and also a little bit through time. It should have taken six hours. I never found out exactly how long it did take, because I wasn't sure what time we left Wrexham. Blisters and Lloyd slowed us down, but stories passed the hours. Aurelia told me about growing up an only child on a pony farm and I told her about growing up a big sister in a huge international city. We traded tales of our first-year roommates and first boyfriends, our first times getting drunk, and our finest hours winning Kahoots in front of the whole class. We got sidetracked by a long discussion about British versus Canadian frats, and I told her how to make Irish cream in a blender and she told me in detail how to birth a foal. It was your typical uni girl late-night gab, except punctuated by counting hill forts. And then we were descending, footsore, empty of soda bottle and full of bladder, loopy with relief, toward the headlights flashing Morse code for "Aurelia, You Idiot" in the Moel Fenlli car park, and tumbling into the passenger seat of Rhiannon Ambrose's battered silver truck.

Chapter 13: Mom, Can I Keep Him?

"Llan-fair-pwll-gwyn-gyll-go-ger-y-chwyrn-drobwll-llan-tysilio-gogo-goch," said Rhiannon. "Come on, Canada, say it with me."

"I hear four L's in a row," I said. "I can't even do two." I was squashed against the window on the passenger side, watching the lamps on Britannia Bridge strobe across the side mirror. "What's it mean, anyway?"

"Saint Mary's church in the hollow of the white hazel near the fierce whirlpool of Saint Tysilio of the red cave."

The parental eruption had taken place between Moel Fenlli and Ruthin. There'd been aftershocks from Ruthin to Trefnant, which had subsided to grumbling by the time we hit the coast. Cod fillets and chips at a 24-hour chippie in Colwyn Bay went a long way toward restoring Rhiannon's sense of humor. Mine remained unrestored, because the eruption had only been about having to rescue her daughter from the middle of nowhere at two in the morning. I wasn't sure what was going to happen when Aurelia opened her backpack. I *was* sure I wanted to be several counties away when it did.

The backpack currently sat at my feet, as far from the hot air vents as we could get it. I'd discreetly slipped half a cod fillet in there while Rhiannon was consulting Google Maps, which had kept him fairly quiet.

The truck rolled off the bridge and into the tiny town of Llanfairpiggledywiggledy, home of the longest place name in Wales. Nothing was open. We passed straight through the center of town and turned onto a narrow country rode that wound between hedges and low stone walls. I was half-convinced we were going to round a corner and come bumper-to-bumper with a patrol car, but they must not have figured out who Aurelia was and where she lived, because there was nothing.

As the person closest to the door, I was the one booted out to open the gate. It took me a while to figure out the latch. When Rhiannon drove through, I hobbled back to the passenger door to catch a ride the last fifty feet to the house. I didn't want to walk another step for the rest of the weekend.

Aurelia's house was one of those whitewashed stone boxes with square windows, a square door, and slightly off-kilter corners that could've been thirty years old or a thousand. There was a horseshoe nailed over the door. I wasn't sure if it was an advertisement or a bit of small magic. Rhiannon opened the door and we followed her into a snug kitchen with a muddy tile floor. A patchy farm cat with a crooked tail peeled himself from a kitchen chair and oozed to the ground, stretching.

"Well, here's home," Aurelia said, lowering her backpack with great care into the mound of rubber wellies by the welcome mat. She shifted awkwardly from foot to foot. We hadn't actually rehearsed the Mom-can-I-keep-him speech. That was starting to look like an oversight.

"Aurelia, why don't you take Marlene to your room while I fix you both hot cocoa?" said Rhiannon. "Take the mat from the porch bench if you don't want to share your bed." She looked at me. "As you can see, we don't do fancy around here."

"Hot chocolate would be wonderful—thank you." Given that I'd half-resigned myself to camping in Ty Mawr, a mat on the floor sounded like luxury.

Aurelia hesitated. Her mouth opened. Nothing came out. I caught her eye and jerked my head at the door, trying to wordlessly communicate that we should strategize in her room. Something butted my ankle lightly. I bent down to find the cat rubbing his head against my jeans.

"Hi," I said, bending down to scratch his ears.

"Meet Flat Peter," said Aurelia, seizing on this distraction. "Peter because, well, no particular reason, and flat because he got his tail stepped on by a pony."

Flat Peter, in the manner of cats, lost interest in me as soon as I evinced a willingness to pet him. I managed to stroke his back once before he teetered off to inspect the backpack.

"Come here, Petey," Aurelia yelped, diving after him. She scooped him into her arms. Her mom looked at her oddly. Quickly, she said, "I haven't seen Flat Peter in months. I'm kidnapping him. Mwahaha."

Seeing how this was going to end if I didn't intervene, I hustled her out the door.

Her bedroom was small and full of paperbacks. The floor was covered in laundry that looked like it dated to the winter holidays. She kicked the door shut, dropped

Flat Peter, and threw herself onto her bed. "She's going to kill us!"

"No, she's not," I soothed. "She's going to kill *you*. I'm going to stay here and watch the cat."

Aurelia starfished on her quilt, looking as panicky as she had back at the Sophia Gardens bus station. "What if she says I have to take him back?"

"She likes animals, doesn't she?"

"Well...yes."

"So spin it like this. 'Mom, look at this poor creature who was suffering in Cardiff.' Tell her about the indignities the rugby team put him through, and promise that he's just a big reptilian dog. Hey, I wonder if you could train him like a sheepdog."

She nodded slowly. "Yeah, you're right. That's the way to—"

"Aurelia!" Rhiannon bellowed from the kitchen. "Why is your backpack twitching?"

Aurelia looked like she wanted to crawl under the bed.

A scraping sound traveled our way. The bedroom door flew open. Framed in it was Rhiannon, towing the backpack by the strap. She was a big woman, brawny like someone who spent a lot of time with her forearm up a pregnant pony, and right now she looked ready to snap both our necks.

"Uh...hi, Mom," said Aurelia, sitting up. "Um. Um. Um."

"Don't look at me!" I threw up my hands. "Flat Peter and I are going to go find that bench cushion." I got up, stepped over the backpack, squeezed past Rhiannon, and fled. Flat Peter quite sensibly decided my company was preferable to Rhiannon's right now.

I and the cat stayed outside watching moths flutter around the porch light for about ten minutes. I made friends with him by dint of pretending he didn't exist until he got impatient and began to butt my ankle. When I was pretty sure parental eruption, part two, had run its course, I reached for the doorknob. I cracked the door just a little, listened, heard nothing too alarming, and slunk back inside, holding the long cushion like a shield. Flat Peter stayed outside.

Rhiannon was banging tins around in the process of fixing some really angry hot cocoa. Lloyd lay in pride of place on the kitchen table, gnawing a frozen chicken drumstick. Aurelia skulked in the corner.

"Did you know about the dragon, Canada?" asked Rhiannon.

"Y—no."

"Right answer." She slammed two mugs on the counter and spooned cocoa mix aggressively into them. "*Assuming* the police never figure out where we live, Aurelia still can't take care of a pet dragon. She has school. I don't know how to take care of a dragon. I've never done reptiles. What am I supposed to do?"

She was looking at me, which I assumed—erroneously—meant I was supposed to suggest something. "Take him to the dragon sanctuary?"

She swelled with indignation. "As if I would trust the *English* to take care of him? I wouldn't trust the government to keep a dung beetle alive." She seized the electric kettle like she'd throttle it. "As if I didn't have enough dependents on my land." She sloshed hot water into the mugs.

"He could be a sheepdog," Aurelia said in a small voice.

"Sheep d—*SHEEP DOG?*" she spluttered. "Augh! Useless animal. He'll be lying in front of the radiator three-quarters of the year, and the rest of the time, running about spooking the mares. Sheepdog. Ugh. And what do you suppose I'll feed him? Cat kibble?"

"He could eat the mice in the barn," said Aurelia, at the same time that I said, "Do you have a rodent problem?"

"Now there's a thought." She battered the cocoa into submission with the spoon, but her expression went a shade less filicidal. "Do you suppose he'd like bats? Only, I've had the worst trouble with bat guano in the shed this year."

Through all this discussion of his future, Lloyd lay bonelessly in the middle of the kitchen table as if he'd melted there. His tail dangled over the edge, swishing gently.

"All right," said Rhiannon. "Suppose he pulls his weight as pest control. He can't be any worse than that useless cat of mine. But what's to keep him from wandering over to chew on the neighbors' cows? I don't suppose the Morgans or Jem Roberts will be pleased by their new neighbor."

"Oh," said Aurelia, who clearly hadn't thought of that.

I had, actually. "Um. This might be a North American thing, but do you guys have those dog collars with a range on them? I mean, if the dog goes too far from the little box thing that talks to the collar, it gives him a zap, so it trains him to stay in his own yard."

"Don't zap my poor dragon," said Aurelia.

"That's not a bad thought," said Rhiannon at the same time, grudgingly. She, clearly, had no objection to a bit of shock therapy. "All right. So that's the neighbor problem taken care of. And the flight problem, come to think. I assume the zap box works *up* as well as *out*."

"I have no idea. Probably."

"Mind, I'm not convinced you've seen the last of the police, Aurelia. Even if they never figure out who's in the security footage, they know you're the one who hatched him; they're bound to come out here eventually. What do you suppose I should do if they do?"

Neither of us had a good answer to that. "Hide him in the shed?" Aurelia suggested in a small voice.

"He's the color of a fire engine."

"Revisit the question in the morning?" I suggested.

"That's the first sensible thing to come out of anyone's mouth in a long time." She tossed the spoon into the sink with a loud clatter. "Cocoa's ready when you want it. I don't know about you two, but *I* have to be up in four hours. I'll have my earplugs in, but do be quiet about it when you go to bed." She left us to our cocoa. I brought Aurelia her mug. We sat on the windowsill.

"That could have gone worse," I said.

Aurelia took a deep breath and released it by blowing on her cocoa. "*Way* worse," she said, with feeling.

The cat door creaked. Flat Peter oozed inside. I could practically hear his eyes latch onto the twitching tip of Lloyd's tail. On silent paws, he padded across the tiles.

"Well, that's it, then," I said. "An end to your quest. You win."

"*We* won."

I rolled my eyes. "You evaded half the policemen in Wales, outsmarted a net of police barricades, *and* vanquished your fire-breathing mother. I was just along to navigate."

We sipped our hot cocoa. I pictured the conversation as a volleyball that rolled away and that we were both too tired to chase. It was two in the morning. My eyelids were heavy, and lots of little aches that I'd been ignoring bloomed to colorful life. That cushion and comforter on the floor of Aurelia's room started to sound like heaven.

It was just as we were both nodding off over the dregs of our cocoa that all hell broke loose.

I hadn't been watching, but it wasn't hard to guess what'd happened, given the combination of cat and twitchy dangling dragon tail. There was a shrill teakettle squeal and an outraged yowl, and then there was a scaly and furry dervish bowling around the kitchen floor. Aurelia yelped and leapt up on the chair, which proved futile when the tangle of claws and teeth and lashing tails went airborne. Lloyd's random wingbeats generated a windstorm that knocked the roll of paper towels off the counter, swept flowers out of the jar on the windowsill, and set the blinds clattering.

"Oh, stop it, stop it!" Aurelia yelped. "Lloyd, you awful lizard, leave him alone! Peter, quit it, cut it out! Somebody do something!"

I looked around for somebody who would do something. The indomitable Rhiannon failed to appear in the doorway. Lloyd and Flat Peter caromed off a cabinet. The doors rebounded open, and several plastic bottles fell out.

Lloyd's lashing tail whipped my ankle in passing. It hurt.

"Make them stop!" Aurelia wailed, practically in tears.

I spotted a bottle of Windex. I started toward it, but had to jump up on the counter and yank my feet out of reach as Lloyd and Flat Peter whirled by again. I didn't want to get caught in the crossfire. There were claws everywhere.

Lloyd was doing most of the flailing, and at first, I thought it meant he was the one in distress. But something was bothering me, and eventually—time moves slower in the face of violence; it was probably only a few seconds, but it felt like I'd been watching for whole minutes—I realized what had turned my stomach inside-out, and that was that Flat Peter had gone awfully quiet after the first bout of hissing. Notwithstanding that he'd started it, all of a sudden I realized how much longer Lloyd's claws were, how much longer his neck was, and just how many teeth were crammed into that mouth of his. And as I turned my back on him to reach for the Windex, I heard the most godawful wet crunch.

I seized the neck of the bottle and spun around. Aurelia was flapping her hands and hyperventilating. I sighted down my arm and pumped the trigger. A fine pink jet of Lavender and Peach Blossom disappeared into the warring knot of animalia. I reached behind me and grasped at random, and came away armed with a pancake spatula. Feeble weapon with which to battle a dragon, if he decided to take umbrage at the squirt bottle, but instead he dropped Flat Peter and slunk sullenly under Aurelia's chair.

Flat Peter just kind of lay there.

Aurelia was gasping. I realized the hairs on the back of my neck were standing up. The entire thing had taken forty seconds. And as my eyes met Aurelia's, I knew those forty seconds had changed things.

Chapter 14: A Hollow Hill for Lloyd

There was blood. I don't mind blood, and neither did Aurelia, usually, but it's different when it comes from something helpless and furry that you're supposed to be responsible for. All I can say is, thank God for the nine lives of cats. Flat Peter peeled himself up, evaded Aurelia's grasping hands, and wove punch-drunkenly between her legs and out the cat door. I was busy holding Lloyd off with the chair, so I couldn't help. Aurelia swung the door open and gave chase, but she was back in less than a minute empty-handed, because "What if he has a broken rib and picking him up makes it puncture something?" I could tell she'd grown up around livestock. "He got away. There are a million places he could be hiding. I'll never find him in the dark. I'll have to try again in the morning."

With Flat Peter out of the picture, Lloyd calmed down. His neck curved sheepishly. He looked up at us with big eyes and a tilt of the head. That wasn't going to cut it. I wouldn't forget that teakettle hiss in a hurry.

"Should I wake Mam?" Aurelia said.

"I'm not sure why you're looking at *me* to know what to do." With Lloyd's wings drooping in that abject way, the chair started to feel like overkill. I put it down. My ankle was really hurting. I sat and rolled up the leg of my jeans. "I'm also not sure what your mom could contribute. Is there even a vet hospital open this late?"

"No," Aurelia admitted.

"How did he look?"

"At least he was walking. I don't know. I was afraid to touch him."

We surveyed the mess. Lloyd's wings had blown paper towels, flowers, and the dish scrubby around the room; one of the cabinet doors hung funny; there was a puddle of Windex and some sticky red footprints on the tiles. In truth, there wasn't *that* much blood, just a couple of drops that'd got smeared so they looked like murder.

I inspected my ankle. A red welt half-encircled it where his tail had whipped me. It stung like sunburn. Definitely not fatal. "And...*how* much more is he supposed to grow?"

She pulled out the other chair and fell into it like her puppet strings had been cut. Her head dropped into her hands, and she didn't answer. Lloyd's nails scritched gently on the floor as he waddled over to sniff her foot. She flinched and moved it out of his reach. I knew she was thinking what I was thinking, which was that if he could do that to a cat tonight, what could he do to a pony in a few weeks? Or a person?

I got up. I dipped one of the paper towels in the pool of Windex and went to work on the smeared red footprints. I wasn't sure why. Cleaning up cat blood spilled by a dragon at 2:23 a.m. in somebody else's house wasn't a requirement on the roommate survey. But I didn't know what else to do. I couldn't picture Aurelia doing it, and I couldn't stomach the idea of leaving it there all night, cooling and going flaky at the edges. Morning seemed a long way off. When I was done, I balled up the paper towel and buried it deep in the waste bin where the blood wouldn't show. I don't know why I did that, either. I wasn't planning not to tell Rhiannon what'd happened. I just didn't want to look at it.

Aurelia's voice was tiny and breathy, and she spoke into the palm of her hand. "If that had happened in Cardiff, they'd probably have a serious talk about putting him down."

There wasn't anything to say to that. She was right. Everybody had been acting like he was a pet, even us. He wasn't.

"So," I said. "What now?"

She pulled her feet up onto her chair and sat cross-legged. Lloyd, deprived of anything to lick in abject apology, lay down coiled around a table leg. In a small voice, she said, "We can't return him to the rugby team. He'll do it again, only this time, it'll be somebody's dog or a toddler, and there'll be cameras, and they'll kill him, or at least lock him up forever and ever and never let him out."

"Yeah," I said.

"But we can't just release him into the wild. There isn't enough wild."

She was right about that, too. He knew people meant food and warmth. The national parks just weren't big enough to keep him away from them. With most of the hollow hills gone, destroyed by mining and urban spread, he'd be stuck aboveground. He'd keep coming up to the tourists looking for handouts, and the bigger he got, the more dangerous that would become for everybody involved.

In an even smaller voice, she said, "It's going to have to be the sanctuary, isn't it?"

"I think so," I told her.

"You've been there. Is it nice?"

DragonWorld Blaenau Ffestiniog was a private zoo in an old slate quarry. The dragons lived behind glass in rock gardens with spray-painted lichen. For seventy pence you could buy a handful of kibble to feed the hatchlings in the petting pen. In the portrait booth there were plumed helmets and wooden shields that you could don to get your picture taken with a mellow old toothless dragon in a muzzle.

"He'll love it," I said wanly.

"Uh-huh." Aurelia eyed me over the top of her hand.

I dragged myself up from my chair and limped over to my backpack. Truth be told, I was a little wary as Lloyd's head tracked my movements. I felt as if I read something sinister into his eyes that hadn't been there before. I dragged my laptop out of my bag and brought it back to the table. "What's your Wi-Fi password?"

She gave it to me. I got my laptop online and looked up DragonWorld Blaenau Ffestiniog. The connection took forever, and half the pictures came up blank. I pulled up their website and turned my screen around so she could scroll through the ones that did manage to load.

She wilted.

"So?" I said. "What do you think?"

I was proud of her for not crying, even though I could tell she wanted to.

Chapter 15: The Hound of Annwn

As an end to Aurelia's hypothetical fifth branch of the Mabinogi, it was ignominious. Aurelia objected strenuously to the muzzle, but Rhiannon was adamant. Getting it onto Lloyd at seven the next morning involved opening all the windows and doors in the house and waiting till he turned into hypothermic treacle, then distracting him with a frozen sausage at the end of a pair of tongs while Rhiannon snuck up from behind. The tongs were probably overkill, but once we'd told her what'd happened, she'd gone all safety-mom.

Opening the windows had the side effect of letting in the soupy fog. We sat around the table eating a clammy breakfast of Weetabix—Lloyd was the only one who got sausage—in an equally frigid silence. Aurelia was quiet and withdrawn because she didn't want to let Lloyd go. Rhiannon was quiet and angry because there was a hypothermic dragon on her floor. I was quiet, too, because I didn't have anything useful to say, and it was seven in the morning after a very, very long night.

We couldn't leave for Blaenau Ffestiniog right away, because farms don't work like that; there were ponies and chickens to feed, stalls to muck, and Flat Peter to track down in the barn and inspect in case he needed to go to the vet, which Rhiannon decided he did, because he was huddled in the hay with his fur all matted. The fact that she got him wrapped in a blanket and stuck in the cat carrier without further bloodshed (hers, I mean) confirmed it. She called ahead to the vet.

While she was gone, we made ourselves useful. A farm generates endless ways to keep busy. Aurelia embarked on a project to reorganize all the tack in the equipment shed. I helped clean little fiddly things that went in ponies' mouths. It was a good way to distract ourselves. While we were at it, we jury-rigged a dragon-sized harness and leash.

*

Rhiannon was back in the early afternoon, sans Flat Peter. The vet had stitched him up and was keeping him for observation. He was pretty thoroughly beat up, but probably not in serious danger. The direst wounds had been to his dignity. When Aurelia heard that he'd be okay, she hugged her mom.

"Canada, you're navigating," Rhiannon said as we gathered our coats and shoes. "Get us to Blaenau Ffestiniog."

Backing Lloyd into the horse trailer was a lot harder than getting Flat Peter into the carrier; there was a great deal of hissing and tail-lashing, and hypothermic or not, we were all crisscrossed with welts by the time the metal door slammed behind him. He was in the smaller of two padded pony stalls, and Rhiannon had tethered a doggie bed to the floor where it wouldn't slide around. Aurelia fixed up a water dispenser with a spout, like the kind my brother had for his rat, but Lloyd didn't seem sure what to do with it.

I didn't see any more of Llanfairpiggledywiggledy on the way out than I had on the way in, because the fog was dense enough to bottle. Aurelia angled all the heat vents in the truck to blow directly onto us, but it was one of those damp days that gets into your bones. Rhiannon hooked her phone up to the car radio and played listless New Age harp music as we drove.

The plan was simple. Rhiannon would drive up to DragonWorld. She'd tell the director that she found Lloyd wandering around her land and that he'd mauled her cat. That would make sure the sanctuary people would take him seriously without—hopefully—looking any further for the girl in the security footage.

If you're wondering why Aurelia had to be along for this: so was I. Her mom and I both tried to talk her out of it, but Lloyd was her responsibility, and she wouldn't be parted from him. Rhiannon (no stranger, I figured, to that feeling of responsibility) agreed to let her come along as far as the edge of Blaenau Ffestiniog. She'd drop us off someplace where we could get tea and hide from the rain. My job, at that point, would be to field the meltdown.

*

Blaenau Ffestiniog lay in the heart of Snowdonia National Park. ("Named for Snowdon, the mountain," Aurelia told me as we turned off the motorway.

"You don't have mountains in Wales," I said. "You have large hills."

"So what's a mountain, in Canadian terms?"

"If it's got snow on the peak in July, it's a mountain.")

Snowdonia was a landscape of crumpled granite and smashed slate. Barren outcroppings stood sentinel over dark valleys cupping electric blue lakes; I knew because I'd seen the postcards. Outside the window, the fog twined eerily, sometimes folding shut so we could hardly see thirty yards ahead, other times parting abruptly to reveal sheer slopes or lone trees or white brooks that burst from the rocks, tumbled down deceptively deep streambeds, and vanished again.

The map on my phone, which I'd managed to charge with Rhiannon's spare plug, took us down one-lane roads where muddy sheep grazed in stony pastures. They huddled miserably together, their fleeces swollen like sponges. Where there weren't pastures, the hillsides disappeared into murk. Their scree-covered flanks were softened by a furring of chartreuse lichen. The fog smeared all colors except the lichen into a matte gray. Most of the time, we were the only thing on the road, but occasionally a pair of headlights materialized like will o' the wisps, barreled down on us, and then raked past and were swallowed up.

Google Maps told me that the drive would be fifty-four minutes. A hundred and twenty-six minutes later, Rhiannon conceded that we were lost. It wasn't entirely my fault. Welsh national parks aren't big on road signs or cell service.

"Aurelia, put the address into your phone," Rhiannon said. "We'll see if we get a different answer."

We did, but another forty minutes later, we concluded that it had also been the wrong one. It didn't help that none of the three phones in the car would keep a signal for more than five minutes.

"New plan," announced Rhiannon. "We drive straight until we hit civilization, then ask a local for directions. Canada, you're the tourist; you can do the talking."

"That sounds like my kind of plan," I said.

So we drove. And drove.

There's a reason that the Princes of Wales were also Lords of Snowdonia; the place is something in the order of eight hundred square miles, easily a kingdom in its own right, if one that wasn't useful for growing anything but roof shingles. Hills loomed and disappeared. We passed through a grove of black trees once, then never saw it again, even though I could've sworn we were going in circles. Low drystone walls rolled up and down the slopes, half-crumbling so that the stones they shed were indistinguishable from the stones shed by the hills themselves.

I'm not sure exactly when my phone dropped its last bar, but we never found another. Rhiannon's and Aurelia's had given up miles ago. We rolled on through the flat gray afternoon. We stopped once for bathrooms at a little car park at the foot of a hiking trail, and let Lloyd out to pee behind a bush. He was so cold and carsick that he didn't even make a break for it. We would have stopped again for food, if there had been any, but for long stretches, we could've been the last four souls in Britain.

For a long time, none of us commented on the banging. I assumed it was a sound Rhiannon's truck always made, because if it wasn't, she would have said something. Aurelia thought it was the bodhrán in the background of the Celtic album. Rhiannon thought it was Lloyd scrabbling around in the trailer. None of us thought twice till an unhealthy hacking cough joined the chorus.

"Shite," said Rhiannon.

"You mean that's not a normal truck sound?" I said.

"Uh-oh," said Aurelia.

Rhiannon flexed her hands on the wheel. "Right. Start praying to the Goddess for a cell bar."

The engine spluttered, died, revived. The weight of the horse trailer probably didn't help; I swear I could feel the truck panting with the effort of hauling it over the muddy gravel. For the last several miles, we'd been threading a narrow gap between two drystone walls decorated with a rainbow of car paint, to which we'd already added more than a few molecules. There was nowhere to pull off. Which was a problem, since even a bike couldn't have squeezed past the horse trailer.

"There!" said Aurelia. "Up ahead. Do you see it?"

A break in the wall on our right, giving way to a track that wound steeply away uphill and vanished into the fog.

"Good eyes, Aurie," said Rhiannon. "I'm going to pull us off there. Otherwise, when the engine goes, we'll cork this whole stretch of road."

So, naturally, thirty feet from the gap, the engine croaked.

We rolled to a natural stop with Rhiannon's front bumper almost—*almost*—close enough to kiss the gap in the wall.

Rhiannon said several things in Welsh that probably touched on the truck's parentage, IQ, and choice of romantic partners. She finished by whacking the steering wheel with the side of her fist, which honked the horn. She turned the key in the ignition. Nothing, not even a faint splutter, not even when she took it out and stuck it back in. The parking lights were on and the dashboard was still lit up, and the problem wasn't the gas tank, unless the meter behind the wheel was lying to us.

"What now?" I asked.

Rhiannon took a deep breath. "I don't know where we are. Can either of you spot a street sign? A trailhead?"

We all craned to see up that muddy track. Nothing.

"There could be a house up there," said Aurelia hopefully.

"Or there could be a trail that goes for miles and miles with nothing but scenic outlooks," said Rhiannon, but she was already reaching for the door handle. There was no room to open the passenger door. We all had to squeeze out her side. Tendrils of fog licked around the top of the window. The gravel crunched wetly underfoot.

"What now?" asked Aurelia as we all shuffled sideways around the car, trying not to scrape our jeans on the wet wall. "Straight, or up the trail?"

It was hard to tell narrow highways from broad trails around here. There could be a house cupped just out of sight in the fold of the hill, or even a whole town; or there could be nothing but wilderness.

"Even if it's a trail," I said doubtfully, "there'd have to be a car park up there; the hikers have to put their cars somewhere, right? And if there's a car park, the trailhead sign might be up there instead of down here."

It wasn't like we had an abundance of choices. Rhiannon nodded. "We'll give it ten minutes. If we don't see lights by then, we'll turn around and come back to the car. I don't want to be lost in Snowdonia overnight."

"What about Lloyd?" asked Aurelia.

"Better bring him."

She had to climb up on the wall and walk along the top to get past the horse trailer. We could hear her cooing to Lloyd as she coaxed him into the jury-rigged harness and leash. Then she lifted him from behind like an extremely floppy cat and laid him on the wall. He rose on the tips of his claws, probably trying to keep as much of himself off the cold slate as possible, and refused to move an inch in any direction.

"Come on, Lloyd-boy," she cooed. "Come on, you sweet lug, we'll find someplace nice and warm for you, and a hot sausage, but you gotta work for it..."

We didn't have any food to bribe him with; we'd planned to have him ensconced at DragonWorld by now. I saw a battle ahead. But then his tongue flicked out, tasting the air, and he must have tasted something he liked, because all of a sudden he was off like a shot, skittering down the wall and leaping onto the hood of the truck with his wings flopping and his claws scratching the paint.

"Come back!" Aurelia yelped, scrambling after him. She'd lost the leash. Rhiannon seized his harness like the straps on a grocery bag and hauled him off her truck. She held him, squirming, two feet off the ground, till Aurelia slid down on our side and reclaimed the leash. She tried to scratch his head, but he wove it side to side, tongue flicking. "What's got into you, Lloydbucket?"

Rhiannon put him down. He walked to the very end of his leash and stood there expectantly, not quite towing Aurelia but certainly making it known that he would like to head uphill at her earliest convenience. Rhiannon locked up the truck. We started climbing, Lloyd leading the way. The trail was mostly mud, a little slippery, and it trickled uphill like a creek in reverse. To either side, the slope was made up of loose scree held together by a tattered cloak of lichen. The fog shifted restlessly over our feet and twined around our legs. It tumbled and whorled playfully in the contours of the hillside, forming shapes you could almost put name to, then flaking apart into meaningless wisps. That's why, when the shape coalesced, I couldn't swear it was real.

Lloyd stiffened. He started to rumble low in his throat.

"What is it, Lloyd-boy?" asked Aurelia, scanning the slope around us.

I tapped her on the shoulder. Silently, I pointed.

"Oh," she whispered.

It was silhouetted against an outcropping, or we never would have seen it. Sleek and white from nostrils to tail, except for the russet tips of its ears, like something that'd stepped out of the Otherworld.

Rhiannon had marched ahead of us by then. She was almost hidden by the contour of the slope, so for a few seconds, it was just us frozen on the path with Lloyd quivering over our feet, and all of us staring at the otherworldly hound.

"That isn't..." Aurelia whispered. "You know..."

"I don't think so," I murmured. "All dogs look the same in the mist."

"If there's a dog," Aurelia whispered—the slope seemed to call for whispers—"There's got to be an owner somewhere, right?"

The greyhound didn't come any closer—probably smart, with a territorial dragon wound around our feet—but his tail flicked once, not really a wag, but definitely an acknowledgement. Then he turned round and melted away uphill.

"I know where we are," I said suddenly.

Lloyd surged up the trail, practically dragging Aurelia. I wasn't sure if he was chasing the dog or only following it, but he seemed intent on reaching the end of the path. We caught up with Rhiannon over the next rise, and we all froze, even Lloyd, and stared at the tower.

It was more scaffolding than tower. If you weren't an archaeology student, and your eyes didn't pull toward old things like the needle graphic on your screen pulls north, the first thing you noticed might've been the white open-sided pavilion with the plastic table under it, or the sturdy, mud-splattered red sedan parked under the one pine tree, or all the orange plastic tape strung between the stakes marking out a generous square around a circular hole in the ground. Those might be what Rhiannon and Aurelia and Lloyd noticed first. But I recognize castles like normal people recognize faces.

It'd taken considerably more than the five bus transfers and seven hours and fifty-five minutes that

Google had promised, but I'd made it to Vortigern's Tower.

151

Chapter 16: It's A Smaller Country Than You Think

A figure emerged from the mist, like a goddess from the Otherworld, if goddesses wore turquoise wellies and leather utility gloves and carried sheets of plywood under one arm.

"Dr. Gilda!" I said. And then I started laughing and couldn't stop.

She stared at Lloyd. And stared. And stared. And finally said, "Long story?"

*

Introductions all round.

"I found him in my barn," said Rhiannon, striking an artful balance between indignation and bemusement. For somebody so salt-of-the-earth, she was, like Aurelia, an impressive liar. "I was trying to drive him to Blaenau Ffestiniog, to that sanctuary, what's it called, where the American tourists go. I figured they'd know what to do with him. My daughter and her roommate wanted to come along, you know young girls and cute animals. If I'd known we'd have so much trouble, I would've called pest control to come fetch him instead."

I couldn't tell if Dr. Gilda swallowed the story. It depended how closely she followed the news and whether she connected the girl in the vegan leather jacket in the security tape with the girl in the fuzzy cardigan standing in front of her. It was just possible that out here, she hadn't been touched by the media storm of the last twenty-four hours. She looked exhausted, like most of what she'd been doing in the last twenty-four hours had involved plywood and duct tape.

Me, though, she remembered. When she said so, I put my face in my hands. "As the girl whose phone went off in class twice?"

"Oh, I'd forgotten that," she said. "No, as the girl with the Roman helmet sticker on her laptop apple. I had decal envy."

She couldn't take her eyes off Lloyd. The look she gave him wasn't the look of a fan meeting a superstar, or of a good citizen meeting a chunk of reward money. She bit the inside of her cheek. She looked wary. Well, I thought, that was reasonable; Lloyd was all trussed up like a pit bull, clear sign that he was somebody to be wary of.

"All my interns have gone home for the night," she said, wiping hair out of her eyes with a muddy glove. "I was just closing up. Well, shoring up or bailing anything that looks likely to sink before morning. The northeast corner's looking droopy again. My white dragon was restless last night, and might be again tonight—" (she winked at me, and I guessed she'd forgotten that I hadn't been there for the end of her story) "—so I've got to make one last check of the load-bearing scaffolding. Then I'm off to Ceridwen's Cauldron. Do you need directions out of here? You wouldn't be the first folks to get turned around."

"What we need is a tow truck," said Rhiannon. She explained about the horse trailer. "You don't get bars up here, do you?"

Dr. Gilda waggled her hand side to side. "My interns are keeping two running scores on the whiteboard. One's for whoever finds the most elf arrows, and the other's for whoever spots the most bars."

"How far to civilization on foot?"

She grimaced. "It's a real hike to get anywhere. To the right, the road dead-ends at Ceridwen's Cauldron— that's the pub—and back the way you came, well, you know the last place you saw streetlights? That's the first place you'll find streetlights. I can give you a ride if you need."

"I'd hate to put you to any trouble," said Rhiannon.

"It wouldn't be any."

It was, on the other hand, as occurred to all of us at more or less the same time, moot. For all intents and purposes, from now until a tow truck came along, our world was bounded at one end by the car park in front of Ceridwen's Cauldron and at the other end by the horse trailer.

"I'm so sorry, Dr. Griffith," said Rhiannon.

"Call me Gilda."

"Gilda. This is my fault. You're trapped here with us."

"Not really. I'm staying at the Cauldron anyway. I'm afraid if I take my eye off this place for more than six hours at a time, I'll come back to a heap of rubble. Girls, why don't you walk your phones around and see if you can find a few bars to call the tow company. Stay off the ground inside that ring of orange tape—that's the well.

Oh, er, better leave the dragon here. Wouldn't want him to fall down it." It was the first time she'd acknowledged Lloyd directly. He was straining quietly but insistently at the end of the leash, his whole body from nose to tail-club forming a straight line pointing at the hole in the ground. Aurelia handed him off to her mom.

I wasn't at all sorry for an excuse to see the tower up close. I'd seen so many photos of Vortigern's Tower in class that actually walking the site felt like déjà vu. Everything was where I expected it to be, even the plastic dustpan that'd been balanced on the lintel in all Dr. Gilda's photos. There was maybe a bit more plywood clamped onto the northeast corner than I remembered. An impressive network of aluminum tubes braced the two standing walls. The doorway—a traitorous piece of my brain wondered if it was really a sixth-century doorway I was looking at, or a Victorian reconstruction— was almost completely filled in with wooden planks, in what looked like a brace of the spit-prayer-and-duct-tape variety.

We circled the tower a few times with our phones out, and then I devised a grid search and we tackled it more methodically. The site wasn't that big. The tower was built in a natural cup in the hillside. It was a clever spot for a fortress, sheltered as it was from the wind but with a good view of the road, at least on a clear day. Boots had churned the ground into a sticky, muddy morass. The ground was waterlogged. Good conditions for the preservation of bio samples like seeds and parasites, but bad conditions for the preservation of architecture. I'd bet that even in summer the ground didn't dry out, because of the way the hillside funneled water into the hollow. No wonder Dr. Gilda was having subsidence problems. I couldn't help snapping photos of the tower whenever I got a good angle, out of the vague sense that I should be preserving it for posterity.

When my bit of the grid search brought me all the way around the tower, I caught sight of Rhiannon and Dr. Gilda leaning on the folding table in the shelter of the white pavilion, chatting while I and Aurelia did the legwork. Dr. Gilda waved to me cheerfully and said loudly to Rhiannon, "It's nice to have minions, don't you think?"

Lloyd's leash was taut. He still stared fixedly at the well.

Aurelia had a false alarm near the far edge of the hollow. "I swear I had something," she told me when I ran up, panting. "Just for a second, there was definitely a bar."

We both waved our phones around like idiots. My fingers were getting cold. We weren't dressed for this. Eventually we gave up. "I think your bar was a ghost," I said.

She shuddered. "I don't want to think about ghosts here."

The one place we hadn't tried yet was inside the tower. I stepped carefully over the stub of the west wall, followed by Aurelia. My shoes almost skated out from under me; the ground inside was soup. My socks squelched. In one corner sat something that looked like a large vacuum with hoses running out of it. I figured it was some kind of water pump.

"This is the kind of history you like, isn't it?" said Aurelia, bending to run a hand along the top of the wall like she was hoping she'd glean some of the appeal. "The 'ancient hands laid this' kind."

"Yeah," I said, and then couldn't resist adding, "You know how you can tell it's Welsh?"

"It's in Wales?"

"It's square. The Normans built round towers, the Welsh princes built square ones." I flicked her. "When I start lecturing you about your own country, that's your cue to say I'm a nerd."

We both waved our phones around halfheartedly. It was pretty clear that the elusive, endangered creature known as the data bar was staying snug in its burrow.

"I just don't see it," she admitted.

"The bar?"

"The big deal."

"I always feel like walking into a ruin is a little like sitting down in a church. It's like, you've got to get in the right headspace, that quiet one where you're listening. And it's hard when your socks are wet."

In the end, we conceded defeat. Ghostly or otherwise, there were no bars. I, Aurelia, Rhiannon, Dr. Gilda, and Lloyd were all stranded in a world that had shrunk to the size of a tower, a pub and a short stretch of road.

We rejoined Rhiannon and Dr. Gilda. As we all began the walk down to the road, Aurelia said, "Dr. Gilda, aren't you going to call your dog?"

Dr. Gilda looked puzzled. "What dog?"

Chapter 17: Ceridwen's Cauldron

Ceridwen's Cauldron was a snug country pub and inn with a whitewashed front and honest-to-God thatch, encircled on three sides by almost-sheer slate cliffs with their tops lost in the fog. There was a tiny car park in front. As Dr. Gilda pulled into a space, I was relieved to see that there was only one other vehicle there, a white van the right size for hauling industrial quantities of laundry and groceries. Hopefully we hadn't trapped many other people on this side of the horse trailer.

Clearly, Dr. Gilda had been staying awhile, because there was a mug of hot tea waiting for her on the table by the door, already with cream and sugar in it, and a cheerful voice called from another room, "Menu choices tonight are lamb stew or lamb stew, or a vegetarian option of take the lamb stew or leave it. Lamb stew sound good to you, Gil?"

Lloyd made himself at home by scraping the mud off his belly on the boot scrape.

"Are pets all right?" Rhiannon murmured anxiously.

"Oh, certainly," said Dr. Gilda, leading the way inside like she owned the place. She raised her voice. "Hullo, Matt, I brought you some guests."

"Brilliant. I'm going to need a bigger pot."

"The cell reception in the dining room isn't bad," Dr. Gilda told Rhiannon, pointing her through a doorway on the left. "Why don't you work on that tow truck?"

Matt turned out to be a giant Irishman whose head practically scraped the ceiling joists. He did a double take when he saw Lloyd, and asked whether he was "the wee tyke from the news," but readily swallowed Rhiannon's story about finding him on her property. The thing about Rhiannon's honest face was that she could've said she raised unicorns and you would've asked what breed.

The dining room had an enormous hearth that had both me and Lloyd wriggling with joy, Lloyd because it had a crackling wood fire and me because it had a sixteenth-century stone hood.

"Not a reconstruction?" I said, getting up close to admire the coat of arms picked out above the bevel.

"Not a reconstruction," Matt promised.

"God, I love this country."

While Rhiannon argued with the tow company, Aurelia looped Lloyd's leash around the table leg closest to the fire. Lloyd curled himself in a mound as close to the grate as he could get, tail wrapped around his paws and neck twisted round so that his head rested on his haunches, like a hill made of scales.

Matt disappeared for a minute and came back with a doggie bowl of raw lamb. He squatted on the carpet for a minute or two to watch the celebrity under his roof. Rhiannon apologized profusely for trapping him here with us.

"Not to worry, luv. There's vittles enough in the fridge to withstand a siege, and disruption of the supply lines just goes with the territory. You should see this place when it snows." He crouched to pat Lloyd, who coiled in a tighter knot and watched the giant hand balefully.

The evening was too murky to say when the sun went down; darkness seeped slowly into the fog till it was more darkness than fog. Matt flipped on the lights. I'd almost forgot electricity was a thing. The fire snapped and popped and made the shadows sway. All the furniture was chunky, handmade, so for whole minutes at a time, you could forget what century you were in.

Rhiannon finally hung up. She glared at her phone for a minute, then mimed throwing it across the room. "Get comfy, girls," she said. "We're going to be here awhile."

Aurelia took Lloyd's muzzle off so he could eat. Rhiannon was poking irritably at her phone. I knew she was fretting about the cost of a night in a boutique historic bed and breakfast, and also about her truck, and Aurelia was fretting about Lloyd, and Dr. Gilda was using that desperately cheery voice that meant she was probably fretting about her sinking tower, so I made a good-faith effort to look fretful too, but the truth was that I was in heaven. I was sitting in a building older than my country, worshipping at the feet of my favorite archaeologist. By the time Matt brought out a pitcher of water and a stack of plastic cups, I'd managed to formulate a question about the tower that made me sound intelligent enough to be worth talking to. "It doesn't sound like there's any other sixth-century sites in the area. What's with the tower in the middle of nowhere?"

It was like asking my brother what video game he was playing; all I had to do after that was sit back and, at random intervals, make small interrogative noises. "That's why the tower is so important," Dr. Gilda said, leaning forward on her elbows. "Because we don't know. The center of the kingdom of Gwynedd should be two hundred miles away, but here we have a stone building, which you know is like a unicorn in sub-Roman Britain, and we have shards of wine amphorae imported all the way from the Mediterranean, and that says to me *royal center.* But there's nothing outside the hollow—I mean, *nothing,* no postholes, no graves, no midden, nowhere to pasture livestock. I've had LiDAR, I've had interns with metal detectors. It's like these people were—not ghosts, they were very real, their chisel marks are real, the Mediterranean wine they drank was real—but like they dropped out of thin air, ate and drank and lived and died in about a hundred square meters for fifty years, and then melted back into the slate."

There was a reason her Netflix specials were so good. As she warmed to her theme, she sketched the whole kingdom of Gwynedd for me, and the tribes, the Ordovices, the Gododdin, the Deceangli, who lived in the ruins after the legions withdrew, and their kings, who built something new out of the ashes of the Roman empire, and who fought each other, and fought the Picts, and peeped over Offa's Dyke, and carved waystones, and raised churches, and composed hundreds of lines of epic poetry that existed nowhere except in the memories of their poets. She could take arrowheads and a bent gold brooch and some postholes in the ground and use them to reconstruct a whole world. But it was a wooden world, and an oral one, and wood rots and oral stories are a centuries-long game of telephone that sometimes loses the signal. Despite what Hollywood tells you, the Dark Ages aren't dark because of plague and war; they're dark because we can't see into them. "And my tower could change that," Dr. Gilda said. "Just a little bit. It's just a small candle in a room so big we'll never see the corners, but we have a chance to see a bit of the floor, maybe, a bit we wouldn't otherwise. But I need more time. Welsh Heritage won't renew my grant; they'd never get tourists up that hill, and two walls and a well aren't flashy enough for postcards. And the scaffolding company won't come out pro bono. I got two professors of terrestrial thaumaturgy to do what they could to firm up the ground, but, well, the west wall is a foot lower today than when I started. I got the BBC interested in doing a fifteen-minute special, but by the time they scrape together the initiative, my tower will be a mound of rubble." She smiled crookedly. "Not that I'm preaching to the choir, or anything."

I nodded, mesmerized.

She lowered her voice. "I have a theory. Welsh Heritage laughed at me."

"What is it?"

"I think there's a dragon under the hill."

"Seriously?"

"Seriously. This whole area's riddled with caves, and there *are* wild dragons. Though most of them are brown scuttlers about this big." She spread her hands. "It'd take a dragon bigger than that to shake the earth, obviously, and in theory, a dragon that big would be in the Snowdonia Wildlife Office's register, but who knows? Maybe he's been hibernating since before Snowdonia Wildlife Office was a twinkle in Parliament's eye, and setting a bunch of interns loose to stomp all over his ceiling woke him up."

I think I was supposed to take that as a joke. I smiled.

"That's why we call it Vortigern's Tower, you know. Have I told you this story? I think I told you this story."

"Actually, I had to leave before—"

But then the stew arrived, and everybody perked up, and the subject dropped.

The lamb was so tender it fell apart, and there were cheese toasties to dip. The conversation moved on; Dr. Gilda and Rhiannon picked up the conversation they must've left off back at the tower, which involved grant applications, archaeological and agricultural respectively, and then somehow, with the male ego as a conversational hinge, took a left turn into the territory of romantic exploits in their own uni days, which made Aurelia squirm. To escape, she and I split off into a side conversation about lamb stew and wok pans and the feasibility of recreating the former in the latter. Lloyd fell asleep.

I didn't hear anything else about Vortigern's Tower that evening, and much later, as we all trudged off to our rooms, the bit that stuck with me wasn't any of Dr. Gilda's storytelling, which had sounded almost ready for the BBC's cameras, but something she'd said right at the beginning. "I'd do anything to save that tower," she'd said, in a tone that reminded me of Aurelia.

It was the off season. Matt's prices wouldn't have anybody mortgaging the farm, but Aurelia and I were still sharing a room with twin beds. It was a rustic arrangement, no other sticks of furniture in sight. We took turns in the bathroom, although she didn't have a toothbrush. At least the room was blessedly Lloyd-free. Lloyd had stayed in front of the fire, safely tethered to the table. Aurelia set her alarm for two in the morning.

"Why?" I groaned.

"That's about how long Lloyd's bladder lasts." She sprawled across her bedspread facedown. "I'll take him out, let him pee, bring him back. You won't even notice, I promise."

"Ugh," I said, and slapped the light switch. With the light out, the room was black as the inside of a dragon's belly. No light pollution outside, I guess.

We both lay there in the dark. Crawling under the covers in jeans felt funny, but I was cold, and the rustling on the other bed told me Aurelia was doing the same.

"Actually, it's not his bladder," Aurelia whispered.

"What isn't?"

"The alarm. The reason I set it. Sorry. I'm tired. What I mean is, I want to check on him. To make sure he's still there. I would have brought him in here with us, but Mam wouldn't let me."

Thank you, Rhiannon, I thought, but said, "Why wouldn't he still be there?"

"Oh, probably nothing. It's just..."

"Yes?"

"I was listening to you and Dr. Gilda. I didn't mean to eavesdrop, but you were a lot more interesting than Mam and the tow truck company. Sorry. Anyway, Dr. Gilda thinks there's a dragon under her site, right?"

"I think she was joking."

"I don't know. Maybe. There's a myth about a red dragon and a white dragon fighting. I don't know, it's just something I absorbed somewhere, but I thought, I'm pretty sure the red dragon wins, so what if she wants Lloyd to fight her dragon and kill it and save her site?"

I rolled over to face her. I almost wished for light pollution; it would've been nice to address myself to a lump in the darkness instead of a completely disembodied voice. "Aurie, that's got to be the most addlebrained conspiracy theory I've heard. If she's trying to save her tower, two dragons fighting under it is the last thing she'd want. Remember how she didn't want Lloyd anywhere near the well?"

"Good point."

"Also, I don't think her dragon theory holds up. If there was a dragon that big in Snowdonia, they'd never let tourists tramp all over it."

"Yeah, okay." She reached for her phone.

"I hope you're turning off your alarm."

"Hm? Oh. No."

Now I could see her. The blue light from her phone screen lit the bridge of her nose and the ends of her hair. "What *are* you doing?"

"Conspiracy theories. I want to see if they've put my name to that security video yet."

"You'll be up all night worrying."

She typed with one finger. There was a long pause. She sighed. "The Wi-Fi here is crap."

"Well, look on the bright side. If they figure out where you are, and they send patrol cars to arrest you, they won't be able to get past your mom's truck. You're a free woman till the tow people get here in the morning."

"Uh-huh," she said, unconvinced.

I sighed. I reached for my phone, too.

"You can go to sleep, if you want," she said. "I don't want to keep you up."

"That's okay. I want to look up the end of Dr. Gilda's story." I deemed it worth the sacrifice of battery percentage. I Googled "Merlin and Vortigern" and got more results than I expected. I scanned the first hit. "Huh," I said. "'The Red Dragon and the White.' There *is* a story about it. Here it goes. King Vortigern's tower falls down every night, he sends his wise men to find a fatherless boy to sacrifice, the boy turns out to be Merlin, and Merlin says *don't kill me, your tower's falling down because there's a red dragon and a white dragon fighting underneath.* So Vortigern digs down into the foundations, and two dragons come bursting out, a red one and a white one. The white one's a lot bigger, and it almost wins, but at the last minute, the red dragon bites it on the neck and kills it. And the upshot is that the white dragon is the Saxons and the red dragon is the Welsh, and even though the Saxons are currently pushing the Welsh around, Wales will rise in the end. *Now* I get the joke. Vortigern's Tower. I wonder if Dr. Gilda named it that because she thought there was a dragon underneath, or decided there was a dragon underneath because the name was Vortigern's Tower." I stuffed my phone under my pillow. "Good night."

"Huh," Aurelia said hollowly.

Her tone made me rise up on one elbow. "What is it?"

"Oh," she said. "Nothing. Um. It's just...the police got my name."

"What?"

"It doesn't matter. I knew somebody'd recognize me. It's not like I don't have any friends. It's okay. It was bound to happen." She was using that desperately sunny voice again. "But, hey, you're right. They can't get a patrol car past Mam's truck. Maybe we should just stay here forever."

"I'm so sorry."

"It's okay."

I listened to her snuffle quietly in the dark for a long time. I fell asleep before she did.

Chapter 18: Timmy's In the Well

In my dreams, a red dragon and a white dragon sat in the hollow, playing Jenga with the tower, while police sirens wailed in the background. Almost unseen, a greyhound with russet ears melted in and out of whorls of fog. I had a plastic dustbin, and I was trying to bail out the well, because there was a pile of cell bars at the bottom, and I had to get to them to win the contest on the whiteboard. The mist around me whispered *Lloyd, Lloyd, where is Lloyd,* but he was sitting right there, easing the keystone from the door lintel, except he was huge, the size of Clifford the Big Red Dog, and the hollow was bowing under his weight.

At some point, the bars at the bottom of the well began to sing: "*You raise me up so I can stand on mountains/You raise me up to walk on stormy seas/I am strong when I am on your shoulders,*" and when I drifted briefly to consciousness, a canned rendition of Celtic Woman's cover of "You Raise Me Up" was playing on Aurelia's phone.

"Turn that off," I moaned.

"*You raise me up to more than I can be…*"

"Sorry, sorry," she whispered. "Go back to sleep."

I did.

My dreams this time were the lucid ones you get between the time you hit snooze and the time your alarm goes off again. The snooze period on my phone is fifteen minutes, so fourteen minutes and forty-five seconds later my eyes popped open ready for school.

The room was black as the heart of a hollow hill, and Aurelia's bed was empty.

"Aurelia?" I said, just in case she was in the bathroom or something. But the room was silent and still.

I lay back down and closed my eyes, calculating my chances of getting back to sleep. I found myself listening for footsteps in the hallway. Seven or eight minutes inched by. How long did it take to run downstairs to check on a dragon?

Finally I tossed back the covers and swung my feet out of bed. I wasn't quite up to flipping on the light, but I sat for a minute, waiting for that nagging sense of unease to go away, and also for Aurelia to come back. I might as well wait; no point going halfway back to sleep and then being woken up by Aurelia opening the door.

Only, she didn't come back. I reached for my phone. It was almost half past. Did it really take Aurelia half an hour to take Lloyd out to pee? I stuck my phone in my pocket and reached for my shoes. I'd better make sure she hadn't locked herself out.

Outside our room, the hall was short and dimly lit. There was no rail on the stairs. I ran my hand over wallpaper dimpled by the uneven stonework behind it. The stairs didn't creak.

The front hallway was dark, but firelight trickled through the doorway of the dining room. "Aurelia?" I whispered, not wanting to scare her. I tiptoed to the doorway and looked in.

Aurelia wasn't there. I frowned. Was Lloyd?

The fire burned dully in its grate. As I tiptoed around the table, I saw that Lloyd was dozing with his tail wrapped around his feet. His leash straggled across the carpet, chewed down to a few threads; Aurelia had never put the muzzle back on him after dinner. I better not wake him, or he might finish the job and make a break for it. I crouched to check his feet. They were dry. Aurelia hadn't taken him outside.

Feeling even more uneasy, I sat on the carpet. Thinking, at two in the morning, is a clunky and low-tech operation, but I had a distinct sense that something wasn't right. If Lloyd and Aurelia had both been missing, I would've assumed she'd got locked out. But I couldn't imagine what she would have been doing outside without him.

Lloyd's eyelids fluttered, so I got up and left.

I could wake Rhiannon, but I wasn't sure I'd survive the experience. I crept to the front door, unlocked it, and stuck my head out to check, just in case.

The fog had cleared and the overcast thinned to the point where moonlight trickled through. It wasn't much, but it was enough to show me a pool of darkness where the car park was and a pool of emptiness where Dr. Gilda's sedan should have been.

Huh. Mystery solved, sort of. Dr. Gilda was staying here so she could check on her dig site; maybe she'd gone to do that, and Aurelia, for whatever reason, had gone with her.

That explanation felt funny to me. A midnight jaunt to a sixth-century ruin was something *I'd* do, not Aurelia. I tried to justify it. Aurelia might've come downstairs to check on Lloyd; she might've bumped into Dr. Gilda; they might've got talking about Dr. Gilda's white dragon, or about magic, or about people they both knew in the magic department at Cardiff Uni, and instead of breaking off their conversation when Dr. Gilda had to go check on her site, Aurelia might've gone with her. Maybe she thought she knew a spell that could help with the dragon or the shaky ground. But my feeling of wrongness didn't go away. I stayed there in the doorway for a long time, letting in the cold. I didn't know what to do.

Something butted my calves from behind. I looked down just in time to see a red shape slither past my feet.

"No!" I said, stomping instinctively on the end of the trailing leash. "Listen, you perambulatory salmonella factory—"

Raveled threads played out from under my shoe as Lloyd kept walking. I hesitated to grab him; he wasn't wearing the muzzle, and I couldn't help remembering the *crunch* Flat Peter had made in his jaws.

"Get back here," I hissed, chasing after him.

And heard the *wham* of the door falling shut behind me.

I whirled. I tried the handle. Locked, of course.

I turned a dirty look on Lloyd. "Look what you made me do." But I was speaking to his backside as he crossed the car park with singular purpose, headed for the road.

"Where the bloody hell do you think you're going?" I was cold already. I hadn't thought I'd need my windbreaker. I followed him at a fast walk. If I'd sprinted, I probably could have caught up, but I wasn't sure what to do if I did. I went from wondering if Aurelia was at the site to hoping she was, because I didn't want to be the one who had to tackle a dragon behaving weirdly at two in the morning.

He must've still been warm from the fire, because far from his earlier sluggish lurch, he moved now at a purposeful slither, head up and forked tongue flicking. He looked like someone who knew where he needed to be. Not that there were a lot of choices, once the low stone wall constricted at the end of the car park and funneled us onto the gravel road. But something made me think Lloyd wasn't just running *away* from me, but *toward* something. *Please,* I thought, *let it be toward Aurelia,* but I found myself remembering his fixed stare at the well earlier, and the greyhound half-seen in the fog, and I had the uncomfortable suspicion that there was something in the air that he could taste, something invisible to me that'd *stay* invisible till I stepped in it and it was too late.

The bare slopes to either side of the road were frozen black waves, their tops limned with tarnished silver moonlight. It smelled like wet stone and moss. There were no trees, and that meant no night birds; the only sounds were the crunch of gravel and my own panting. The silence and chill made me think of the ancient inhabitants of the tower melting into the slate. On a night like this, it wasn't hard to imagine them melting back out of it, their swords and brooches tarnished, their eyes empty.

A shape reared suddenly out of the darkness in front of me, and I nearly jumped out of my skin, till I realized it was Rhiannon's truck, filling the road from wall to wall. Just in front of my feet, Lloyd feinted right, then twisted around left and shot away up the hill, claws scrabbling on the stony path. At the top, a light warmer and harsher than moonlight lit the edge of the hollow. Taillights. I'd been right; Dr. Gilda had driven out here to check her site.

The taillights were enough to ruin my night vision, but not enough to show me where to put my feet. I scrabbled up the hill after Lloyd, slipping and skidding. Twice I tripped and planted hands and knees in the wet.

"Aurelia?" I called.

There was movement on the slope, but it wasn't Aurelia—it was the greyhound, as ghostly as ever, and somehow more predatory without the fog to soften his edges. He neither approached to greet me nor growled to warn me away, only silently paralleled Lloyd's progress up the slope, like an honor guard. Lloyd ignored him and reached the lip of the hollow, where he paused for a moment, washed in the red taillights. In profile, with his clubbed tail lashing and his wings half-outspread, he looked different—nothing like the stubby little animal Aurelia had stuffed in a backpack yesterday. He looked regal. He looked old. He looked like the flag.

"Aurelia?" I called again. "Are you up there? Tackling the dragon is your job. I'll hold the flashlight and be moral support."

The greyhound, when I looked again, was gone.

There was a low, purring hum in the air. It got louder as I approached. For a moment, I thought it was coming from Lloyd, but it was deeper and harsher than anything that could've come out of something his size. I could feel it, faintly, in my sternum, and in the ground. Then I caught up to him and realized it was Dr. Gilda's car, idling.

We stood at the edge of the hollow, looking again at the tower, which was washed in the headlights so it stood out stark against the slate. Electric light was the wrong kind for this place; it was too harsh, and drew more attention to the bones of the scaffolding than the outline of the tower. The well, fenced off by stakes and orange plastic tape, gaped dark and ominous, and in the sideways light of the headlights, footprints in the mud stood out black.

"No!" a voice shrilled suddenly, making me jump. Dr. Gilda had just rounded the sedan, and she was flapping her hands at Lloyd. "Catch him!"

He wasn't doing anything particularly sinister at the moment, but I reached down and retrieved the muddy end of his leash. I wasn't sure I could hold onto him if he really wanted to go somewhere, but for the moment he was frozen, only his forked tongue moving, his head pointing again toward that hole in the ground.

"Hi, Dr. Gilda," I said, in my calmest, most rational everything-about-this-situation-is-normal voice. "I didn't mean to startle you. Lloyd made a break for it. Is Aurelia with you?"

Dr. Gilda wore a Cardiff Uni pullover and her rubber wellies, all spackled with mud. She was looking at Lloyd like she'd been fleeing from doom and it'd caught up. "Sorry," she said. "I didn't mean to snap. I didn't expect to see you...two...here. I just worry about the well. I wouldn't want him to fall down. It's more slippery than it looks. No, Aurelia isn't with me."

"Really? I can't figure out where else she could've gone."

"I have no idea." She was recovering quickly. "Would you like a ride back to the Cauldron? I just ran the water pump. It should all hold up till morning."

"What's that?" I asked, pointing to a snaky thing running from the doorway of the tower to the well.

"The pump hose," she said.

"Aren't wells *supposed* to have water in them?"

"It gets into channels in the bedrock at night, and when the ground warms during the day, it expands and causes cracks."

That made sense. Almost.

"Let me just unhook the machine, and we'll be on our way," she said. "You stay here with the dragon." She turned to walk back to the car.

Lloyd decided he'd tasted enough air. He started to slither forward. I tried to hang on to the end of the leash, but it was too short and there was no loop at the end and it slid through my fingers. "Bad dragon," I said. "Sit."

He paid this all the attention it deserved.

As I chased him, I realized the hose on the ground didn't look right. It was taut—so taut it'd left a straight furrow in the mud and bit into the lip of the well.

"Uh...Dr. Gilda?" I called.

Lloyd's wings rose straight up. Not like he was thinking about flying. More like he was making himself bigger. His tail lashed.

"Yes?" Dr. Gilda called from inside the tower.

"I think something has hold of the end of the hose."

"It's probably caught on something." A moment later, the hose went slack. She'd unfastened it from the pump.

Lloyd slithered under the orange tape. He stuck his head down the hole.

I had a very odd feeling. I stepped over the tape. Cautiously, I crouched next to him. "Are you trying to tell me Timmy fell down the well?" I asked, only it wasn't really funny, because the smell coming out of the hole wasn't the smell of brackish water. It was hot copper and dust.

"Marlene, get away from there," said Dr. Gilda, emerging from the tower. There was real panic in her voice. "Get the dragon away, too. It's slippery." She was coiling the hose as she walked toward us.

I tensed, reaching for my phone. "I just want to see something," I said.

"Don't," she pleaded. "There's nothing interesting down there."

"Maybe we'll be able to see what the hose is caught on."

She hesitated for a moment, unable to think of an objection. I wondered what was down there that I wasn't supposed to see. I palmed my phone. She coiled the hose around her arm and dropped it over one of the wooden stakes. "I'll sort it out in the morning," she said. "It's too cold and dark right now."

I flicked on my phone flashlight and angled it down the well.

Nothing. The shaft wasn't vertical. Ten feet down, it started to slant, so there was no way to see where the end of the hose went.

Kicking myself for never setting up speed dial, I entered my passcode.

"What are you doing?" Dr. Gilda demanded as I thumbed through my contacts.

"Oh, nothing." I stood up. "Just...wondering where Aurelia is. I'll feel silly if she's back in our room and I'm all the way out here looking for her." I hit *call.*

From the bottom of the well, made tinny by small speakers and garbled by echoes, came the first bars of "You Raise Me Up."

Chapter 19: The Red Dragon and the White

Dr. Gilda and I stared at each other in horror.

"We have to call 999," I said. "Wait. Crap. They can't get past Rhiannon's truck. We have to do something."

It's a mark of how well I knew Aurelia that it never crossed my mind that it might just be her phone down there. No, if anybody could fall down an ancient well at two in the morning, it was her.

"Oh," said Dr. Gilda in a funny voice. "Yes. Right. You're right."

I cupped my hands and called, "Aurelia? Can you hear me? Oh my god, please answer."

Lloyd was nearly quivering, his head stuck as far down the shaft as it could get without his front feet following. Dr. Gilda made little snatching motions with her hand, like she wanted to grab his harness but valued her fingers too much.

"Well?" I nearly wailed, looking to her to be the responsible adult. It was her fault Aurelia was down there. Aurelia had got some garbled idea about Dr. Gilda stealing Lloyd to reenact some ancient story.

Some ancient story. I'd dismissed it. I mean, besides being *crazy,* letting dragons fight under her dig site seemed counterproductive.

"Do you know," Dr. Gilda said slowly, squatting in the mud beside me, "magic is a bit like linguistics? I mean, I only took a few magic classes as electives back in uni, and the field's come a long way since then. But I remember this very distinctly, because it tallied with other things I was studying. Languages change over time, and they change faster in big population centers. That's why speech in some remote hamlets sounds archaic. It's preserved. It still works the way it did hundreds of years ago. You have these pockets of ancient dialect preserved in nooks in the landscape. Old magic is the same way. Magic evolves. For a long time, it was a bit like religion, and now it's a bit like science. Academics write papers on the Old Ways. They're powerful. They're vague. The rules are more slippery. If you pin them to a board and study them, they lose their potency. But if you come at them sideways, holding out your hand, they might come sniff. The Old Ways linger in folds of the hillside, like those dialects. Snowdonia has always seemed to me like a place they could hang on. I had to try."

"What are you talking about?"

"This tower is irreplaceable, Marlene. Not just for the things it can tell us, but for its own sake. I think *that*'s something you can understand. I think most people who study archaeology do it because old things sing to them."

"I get that part. I don't get what that's got to do with my roommate falling down a well."

"I didn't want to do it," she said. "But I was out of options. The pumps aren't doing anything. Even with all the grant money in the world, I can't scaffold the entire hillside. And the terrestrial thaumaturgists—their magic wouldn't take. I don't think the white dragon speaks modern magic. I think he speaks an older dialect. He plays to older rules."

I stared at her. "No way."

"Aurelia was afraid I was going to steal Lloyd, wasn't she?" said Dr. Gilda. "She was looking at the right story, but the wrong chapter. Vortigern's first idea—"

"—was to sacrifice a child without a father. You're crazy. Help me pull her out."

Dr. Gilda leaned back on her heels. "If you don't buy into thaumaturgico-linguistic theory, that's okay. Try looking at it this way instead: once the white dragon has eaten, he'll go back to sleep and stop fidgeting."

And the ground beneath us very subtly quivered.

"Aurelia?" I called, tugging at the slack hose. "Aurie? Can you hear me? If you can hear me, tug three times." I looked around wildly, and my eyes landed on the car. I wasn't strong enough to reel her up on my own, but if I tied the other end of the hose to the bumper, and Dr. Gilda backed it up slowly, we could draw her out. "Aurie? Answer me."

Very faintly, I heard a bleary "...Five more minutes?"

Lloyd, with all the patience of molasses, began incrementally to pour himself over the edge. I grabbed his harness just before he could overbalance. "Help me stick him in the trunk," I said. "I mean the boot. Hurry. Then we'll pull her out."

Dr. Gilda took the end of Lloyd's leash. It was just long enough to reach the nearest wooden stake. She knotted it there.

"That's not going to hold," I said. And like an idiot, I turned my back on her to look for something sturdier.

She shoved me.

The ground was slippery and I was already off-balance. I windmilled my arms. There was nothing to grab. I whacked my shoulder painfully on the sloping side of the shaft, and then both feet hit stone with a bone-jarring impact and shot out from under me. I hit my tailbone hard. I tried to put out my hands to slow myself, and skinned both palms, barked a shin and scraped an elbow, and then the bottom of the well came out of nowhere, slamming into me with bruising impact. My knee collided with something soft that said "Oof!"

"Aurelia?" I panted.

"Marlene?"

"Where's the end of the hose?"

"What hose?"

I fumbled in my pocket. My phone had survived the fall. I had hardly any battery left, but I turned on the flashlight. My hands were shaking. I had a confused impression of rough-hewn slate walls and a wet reflective floor and Aurelia lying with her wrists and ankles tied with orange tape. The end of the hose was around her waist. Dr. Gilda must've used it to lower her.

I stood and knocked my head on the ceiling. "Ow!"

"Where are we?" Aurelia asked blearily. "How'd we get here?"

I gripped my phone in my teeth like a pirate's scimitar to free my hands. I tugged the hose. The other end was only looped loosely around a stake up there, and I wasn't sure it'd take my weight. "Shh," I said. "I'm going to try to climb out."

The curve of the shaft hid the sky from me. All I could hear was Dr. Gilda's shoes squelching above us. "Nice dragon," she was coaxing. "Come on. I have biscuits."

Just as I tugged the hose, it went slack. The coil fell on my head. It was followed by a lightweight wooden stake.

I spat out my phone. "Dr. Gilda?"

"I'm sorry," she called. "I'm really very sorry. I hope you understand. Come on, Lloyd."

"Please don't leave us!"

Her footsteps squelched away. The car door slammed. I heard the engine purr.

"Marlene?" said Aurelia to my feet. "I don't feel good."

I shone my phone down on her. "Are you all right?"

She squinted and looked away. "I feel sort of woozy."

There was blood crusted in her hair. "Dr. Gilda must've hit you over the head with something. What happened?"

"I don't know."

"What's the last thing you remember?"

"I went downstairs to check on Lloyd, only Dr. Gilda met me in the hallway. She said he was gone. She offered to give me a ride to look for him. I figured, as long as I was with her, she couldn't steal him."

"Yeah, no kidding. She was trying to steal *you.*" I clamped my phone between my knees so I could see the orange tape tying her wrists together. It was knotted tight. I picked at the knot with my nails. "A child without a father, huh? Your mom must've told her."

"There's one piece of good news," she said.

"What's that?"

"No giant dragon down here."

I'd forgotten the supposed white dragon. Being shoved down a well and landing on my semiconscious and trussed-up roommate had knocked that clear out of my head. I grabbed my phone and swept the flashlight around us three hundred and sixty degrees. We were in a pocket in the ground barely big enough to call a cave. The floor and ceiling and most of the walls were rumpled slate, except for part of one wall that was a different kind of stone, paler and jagged.

The knot loosened. I worked it free. "Can you sit up?" I asked.

"Is that a good idea?"

"I don't know. D'you know anything about concussions?"

"They hurt." She inspected her ankles. "If you hold the light still, I think I can untie myself."

"This is not how I saw my night going."

"You know what's really funny?"

"What?"

"*Now* she has Lloyd."

"I'd worry more about us."

She picked at the knot. Her chewed-up nails were too short to make any headway.

I handed her the flashlight. "I'll do it."

"Are we going to starve down here?" she asked in a small voice.

"We just have to wait till your mom wakes up, finds you gone, freaks out, and calls the police, and they track our phones, and they find us. Easy. Oh, also, somewhere in there, I guess they'll have to tow the horse trailer."

I got her untied. We wadded up the tape and I stuck it in my pocket, because littering in a priceless historical cave felt wrong to me. After that, we were both at a loss what to do. It was chilly, and we stuck our hands in our opposite sleeves. I thought we looked like monks, and said so, and we both laughed. It's possible we were a little hysterical.

"Well, if you wanted a good climax to your fifth branch of the Mabinogi, this is something," I said.

An eternity crawled by. I kept trying to peer up the well shaft, but I could never quite see the sky. My phone died. Hers still had about two percent battery. We sat in the darkness, conserving the flashlight. One of us had the bright idea of telling ghost stories, till it occurred to us that if we wanted to die here, there were more humane ways to go.

"I can't believe we're doing this," Aurelia said. Her teeth were starting to chatter.

"Doing what?"

"Not panicking. We're wanted fugitives lost down an early medieval well with no food or toilet."

I groaned. "I really wish you hadn't mentioned toilets."

Somewhere in the darkness, stone scraped on stone. The floor fluttered slightly under our feet.

"What if the cave chooses tonight to collapse?" she whispered.

"The site's been doing this for months," I pointed out. "What're the odds that it'll happen *right now*?"

There was a deeper, colder grinding. Water dripped like mad, *plink-plink-plink*. We were clinging to each other pretty hard by the time the ground stopped quivering.

"I want to turn on the light," she whispered.

"I don't know if the police can track dead phones."

Plink-plink-plink went the water, sounding like the footsteps of hollow men.

Light flooded our little cave.

"Just making sure there's nothing awful in here with us," said Aurelia defensively.

There wasn't. Just dirty water on the ground, black slate overhead—and a doorway.

We stared at it.

"Was that there before?" she said.

"Had to be."

"I didn't notice it."

"You were tied up and concussed."

It was just a sliver of space, really, where the paler shingled stone met the slate. Aurelia went to investigate. She had to bow her head to look through. She shone the flashlight ahead of her. "It widens out," she said, voice echoing slightly. "There's sort of a passage."

"Is it headed up or down?"

"Level, it looks like. It curves a little bit, so I can't tell how far it goes."

"There's a lot of survival films that begin, 'Hey, let's go exploring.' So let's not go exploring."

"What if there's a way out?"

"We already have a way out. It's called a fireman's ladder, and it'll be here in the morning."

"You're right." Reluctantly, she turned off the flashlight.

Never underestimate the power of a dark room, an empty stomach, and boredom. For the next hour, they worked on both of us. It was cold, and there was no way to lie down on the wet floor without soaking our shirts. We held an unspoken contest for loudest chattering teeth. We exhaled into the darkness, knowing our breath was fogging invisibly.

"What if the phone tracker thingy can't find us underground?" she finally said in a small voice.

"It will."

"Are you just saying that?"

"Well, even if it can't, how many other places are there to look? Somebody'll find us."

"I read this article once. It was about a hiker with a bone disorder who fell down a mine, and they mistook his bones for an early hominid, except then they carbon-dated them."

"Aurie, nobody's going to mistake us for early hominids. *Maybe* Iron Age shaft burials."

She gulped.

We lasted another half an hour.

"Maybe we should split up," she said. "You can stay here, in case the rescue comes after all, and I can see where that tunnel goes."

"Aurie, there's a whole *other* genre of films that begin 'Let's split up.'" I coiled the hose and slung it over my shoulder like Indiana Jones. "We'll give it fifty paces. If we haven't found a way to the surface by then, we turn around. I really don't want to get lost like that Thai soccer team in the flooded cave."

"Deal," she said. "You go first. There might be spiders."

I shone the light on the ground so we could see where we were stepping. She was right; beyond the narrow entrance, the passage widened far enough that we could nearly spread our arms, and the ceiling vanished. The wall to our left was slate, worn away sheer, and the wall to our right was that pale, shingled stone, rough to the touch and slightly bulging. The air was slightly warmer than in our tiny cave. It smelled like hot minerals.

We'd gone maybe twenty paces when the passage opened out abruptly, the shingled pale wall curving away to leave us at the edge of a cave whose dimensions were lost beyond the edge of the flashlight.

"Uh...Aurie?" I said.

"What?"

I pointed at a veined, curved thing set into the pale wall. It was about the size of my leg. "What does that look like to you?"

"Um...oh...hum." Her voice got progressively smaller. "What does it look like to *you*?"

"A mammoth tusk," I said with more optimism than honesty.

"Mm-hm," she said, equally hopefully. "That's what it looks like to me, too. Maybe a mammoth fell down the well."

Because the other thing it looked like was a very, very large claw.

I hooded the flashlight with my hand. We walked a little further into the open space, which, I realized, was a hollow hill in truth, and the pale stone mound just a bump at its edge. What we'd walked down hadn't been a passage so much as a narrow gap between the mound and the wall of the cave. The mound had odd contours; parts of it folded inward or bulged outward, and it had a long, crooked tail and a long, slack neck.

"There!" Aurelia said, pointing past me.

Across the hollow hill was a pale streak on the wall. It could've been phosphorescent moss. But it could also have been moonlight. If there was moonlight, there had to be an opening somewhere. Beneath the moonlight was a ramp of tumbled rocks. Two enterprising girls with decent shoes and a hose could probably manage to climb it.

"Good eyes!" I said.

"Uh..." She tapped my arm and pointed behind us. "Speaking of eyes..."

I turned.

The thing about an object as large as the pale mound is that it's impossible to see it all in one frame, and so when I spotted the giant eyelid she was pointing to, I couldn't immediately figure out which way its owner's head was facing. The lid was open a crack, and the iris it revealed was salmon-pink, the color of Aurelia's jacket. About two feet below it ran a zipper of mineral-stained teeth, all curved over so brutally that they occupied their own little raw grooves in the warped lips.

"Back up," I whispered. "Back into the little cave. Let's go."

A low rumble started somewhere in the depths of the mound. I spun around and pushed Aurelia from behind. She scurried back the way we'd come, her pullover snagging on both walls, the stone one and the living one. The thing about the pale mound was that it wasn't *scaly.* It was more like bark. You know those trees older than Jesus, the ones that're never as big as you'd expect, but all twisted and gnarled and grown back in on themselves? That was this dragon. The rumble grew gradually. It had a resonance that got inside my head and made my brain vibrate. Water dripped from the ceiling to patter our heads like underground rain. The white mound shifted slightly, scale scraping against slate with a sound to set your teeth on edge. Visions of being splatted like a mosquito against the wall flashed through my head as we dashed back down the narrow corridor and tumbled into our little pocket-cave, splashing down on hands and knees in the floor-sized puddle.

"Did we wake it up?" she whispered under the rumbling. "Or is it just snoring?"

I took a risk and tilted the flashlight back the way we'd come. The entrance to the passage was half as wide as it'd been. From the other side came a slow, ominous scrape.

"I think we should put our backs to the wall and hope its hand—paw—claw—whatever—doesn't fit in here," I murmured.

Watching the shingled flank move against the mouth of our little cave was like watching cold molasses starting to warm up: there was definitely movement, and it started so gradual you could barely notice it, but it was getting a little faster every second, and you knew the more it moved, the more it'd warm up, and the more it warmed up, the more it'd move. We'd set off a reaction when we shone the flashlight into its half-open eye, and now we were reaping the very slow, inevitable consequences.

"If we die," Aurelia whispered, "I just want you to know...you were a really good roommate. Thanks for always doing the dishes."

"We're not going to die. But if we do, you were a good roommate, too. You generated a lot of material for my blog."

"I did? I never read it."

"That's okay. I think the only person who did was my mom."

She made a choked hiccup noise. "If I die here, *my* mam's going to kill me."

Above us, there was a new scrabbling sound. We both looked up. I started to sidle in that direction, not holding out much hope. If rescue was coming, we would've heard the engine and the tires, and we'd be hearing voices. There was nothing but the *scritch* of keratin on slate, and then a sudden flurry of scrabbling and a surprised hiss, and then disaster dropped down the well and almost bowled my feet out from under me in the form of a ball of red scales tangled up in a leash.

Some instinct made me lash out a hand and seize the back of Lloyd's harness. Aurelia gasped. She snatched for the lashing end of the leash. Lloyd was muddy from claws to flanks. His jaws still worked at scraps of orange plastic tape caught in his teeth.

"What the—?"

"Lloyd!" exclaimed Aurelia. "No, stop, stop!"

He was trying to fling himself past her and at the wall of scales. I hauled on his harness. Deep in his chest, he made noises I'd never heard him make before, sort of a grinding croak, like the white dragon's rumble but higher pitched. He lashed his tail in agitation. I stepped lightly on the clubbed end; it was that or let him sweep my legs out from under me.

"What is he *doing?*" Aurelia demanded as his head wove side to side, evading her hands. His paws scrabbled futilely in the puddle. He was as strong as a large dog, and he would've pulled me off my feet if I hadn't leaned back on my heels and hung on grimly. She said, "What are you doing, Lloydbucket? What are you about, hm?"

"Either the world's most mechanically short-sighted mating ritual or a territorial display," I said. "Lloyd, you're the size of that thing's eyeball. I do *not* recommend going for the throat."

He hissed and scrabbled, and from the white dragon in the bigger cave came an ominous rumble.

I'd managed to hang onto Aurelia's phone with two fingers. The flashlight strobed around us, reflecting from the puddle on the floor and making our cave flicker with silent lightning. In its intermittent light, I could see Aurelia's bewilderment. "How did he even get here?" she asked.

"He must've got out of Dr. Gilda's car and circled back," I said. "I want to know *why* he's here."

"Destiny," said Aurelia.

"So it's his destiny to be that thing's midnight snack?"

Lloyd fought. I hung on grimly to the harness. Aurelia managed to catch his head in both her hands. He didn't bite her, just kept trying to see around her, to get line of sight on the other dragon.

"Wait," I said. "Destiny. You're serious?"

"Lloyd—he's been interested in the well since we got here. Mam had to hold him back, remember? And then when you came to find me, what did he do?"

"Tried to stick his head down the well," I admitted. "I thought he was smelling *you*."

"Lloyd, *stop* it!" she said.

My heart was pounding. The white dragon's scales were streaming past the mouth of our little side cave now. It was turning around. I suspected we'd lost any chance of it going back to sleep. It smelled him, too. The scales suddenly vanished, and then the mouth of the cave was filled again by a huge eye, as pink and bloodshot as a lab rat's. Lloyd lunged, all four paws off the ground, and when I didn't let go, he splashed down in the puddle, splattering us all with slimy water. The white dragon groaned low in its chest, making the walls quiver. A fresh shower of mineral-stale condensation pattered down on our heads.

"Marlene?" Aurelia said. "Do you trust me?"

"Nothing good ever started with that question."

"Just answer it."

"Yes," I said. I thought I was lying, but when I reflected on it, I decided not. "Yes, I trust you. Why?"

"Because I want you to let him go."

"What?"

"This is something he has to do."

"How do you know that won't end with all three of us squashed and/or eaten?"

"The same way I knew I had to rescue him from the gift shop," she said. "The same way I knew you'd help me, way back at Sophia Gardens. Maybe the same way the curator knew she had to help us, and the same way the greyhound found Lloyd again. I just do. You don't...*get* magic. You understand other stuff way better than me, like adulting and public transit, but remember the starry-eyed thing, how you didn't get it? I do." She had to raise her voice a little over the clatter of stone. "Trust me. Take the harness off."

"He'll bring the whole cave system down. He'll collapse the tower. On our heads."

"Maybe." She finally managed to clap Lloyd's head between her hands, holding it still. His tongue darted out. It touched the tip of her nose. "Do it now. He won't hold still for long."

I still thought we were likely to end up squashed under tons of falling slate. I took a deep breath. I guess, when it came down to it, I did trust Aurelia. Sort of. In this one thing. I reached under Lloyd's belly and found the buckle. I fiddled it open. Right away he slithered out of the harness, and it splashed into the puddle and disappeared. But he didn't pull his head out of Aurelia's hands. She leaned forward and planted a kiss on his forehead, which might've been an invitation to salmonella, but it was also, in a funny way, a blessing. Then she let him go.

Lloyd flung himself into the hollow hill. I grabbed Aurelia's hand. The eye withdrew as the grumbling growl became a deep, resonant hiss. I towed her after Lloyd, toward that shaft of moonlight, and the exit.

Chapter 20: Milk for the Fair Family

"Aurelia Ambrose, you are under arrest for kidnapping," said the policewoman, and Aurelia, covered in slate dust, with both knees of her jeans ripped, and tear tracks running down her cheeks, and a small, satisfied smile on her lips, held out her hands for the cuffs.

Around us on the slope, the boulders flickered with blue and red lightning. The cop cars were all lined up behind the horse trailer on the road, the size of beetles at the bottom of the slope. In the back of one (I learned later) was Dr. Gilda, also arrested for kidnapping and attempted child sacrifice. Between us and them was a pit full of shattered slate and broken scaffolding.

*

As we'd scrambled up the shifting, sliding ramp of rubble toward that small square of moonlight, the noise behind us had been indescribable. Hissing rebounded through the heart of the hill, sharp as stalactites, and it was impossible to separate the resonant roar of the dragons from the many-layered echo of the scream of their claws on slate. The rock itself quaked like jelly, and musty underground rain pattered our shoulders and slicked the ground beneath our shoes. I got to the top of the rubble first, and found the slit in the ceiling, and boosted Aurelia through it, and then scrabbled up after her. Dust gushed out around us, billowing through the hollow, stinging our eyes and making us cough; and without the headlights to light our way, I never would have found a way out of the hollow, if not for the silvery shape that peeled itself from the blackness. "Aurelia," I said, "look," but she couldn't see it. Its russet ears were pricked. It pivoted and trotted away, and I grabbed her arm and followed. We ran, not looking back, till we found a place where the ground only quivered slightly.

Though I could hardly make out the outlines of the boulders around us, I had no trouble at all seeing the greyhound's sad, wet, ancient eyes as it turned them on me one last time.

"Thank you," I said.

It flowed away between the rocks and was gone.

Aurelia and I stood, panting, and watched the slope heave. We heard slate shatter like glass. We watched the tower totter, held together at first by its scaffolding; and then we watched the plywood splinter, the metal pipes bend, and all at once the tower lost its shape and slumped over like its years of watching over the valley had exhausted it, and then it hit the ground like a breaking wave, and then the whole hillside fell in.

Sticking up from the rubble now was one pale, gnarled claw.

"Marlene?" Aurelia said as the policewoman led her away.

"Yeah?"

"Thanks. For everything."

Somewhere, I found a grin of my own. I was scraped up, too, and hungry, and exhausted, and as scared as I'd ever been in my life, and a priceless tower was smashed to bits small enough to engrave with cheesy slogans and sell in gift shops. "I can't believe we did all that," I said.

"I can," she said.

*

They never did find out what happened to Lloyd. Maybe he got squished. Somehow I don't think so, and neither does the rest of Wales. There's speculation that when it was all over, he just wandered off into a crevice. Those hills are laced with tunnels and caverns and passages. I like to imagine that he found other little dragons, and beat them up, and became a prince of an underground kingdom. I suppose—and so does most of Wales—that he's still down there somewhere, growing to his true size, hibernating and waiting for the day that Wales needs him back. Maybe we'll never know. Maybe Aurelia's right, and fifteen hundred years from now, two girls will sit in the foundations of the Percival Building and write papers on the legend of the red dragon and the white dragon, and of Aurelia Ambrose, who carried a beetle in a baggie and brought down a tower and tamed ponies and made calculators levitate and once stuck a kettle to her boon companion's hand for a whole twelve hours, and was as courageous as she was hapless. Maybe someday she and Lloyd will be one branch of the sort of oral legends that never make any sense, but still make good reading.

Knowing isn't the point. It's the story, isn't it?

*

I made it to Monday lecture on time. That's despite four hours answering questions at the police station in Porthmadog. They let me off. I guess they decided Canadians are too nice to commit felonies, and also, Aurelia swore up and down that I hadn't known about the dragon in the backpack till we were on the train.

The two trials were a media circus. Dr. Gilda got fifteen years in prison. Aurelia got eighty hours of community service. She was expelled from uni. She thought she'd end up a starving vagrant under a bench. I thought so, too. The next morning in her inbox she found seven internship offers and three invitations to apply to grad programs, so I guess she wasn't the only one who thought she'd done the right thing. Anyway, magic programs are the third-most underfunded departments anywhere, after archaeology and literature. Thaumaturgists look after their own.

She signed up to serve her hours at the dragon shelter in Cardiff.

*

Months later, when exams were over and my suitcase was packed and my airline tickets printed, she woke me up at three in the morning.

"You're a big girl; kill it with the wok pan," I muttered, rolling over and dragging my pillow over my head.

"It's not a spider," she said urgently. "Hurry."

I moaned, but dragged my carcass out of bed. I followed her, muttering mutinously, into the hall. She was wearing unicorn slippers and plaid pajamas. Her hair was in rollers. Her eyes were wide. She paused outside her own door. "Be very quiet," she whispered. "Tiptoe. Don't get too close." She eased the door open. "Look."

On the windowsill, three motes of violet light danced around the dish of milk and honey. The summer breeze blew gently across the sill, flickering the candle flame and carrying the scents of hot wax and grass and the sound of soft tinkling.

"The curator was right," she whispered. "I put out a candle. They came."

Quietly, we sat on her carpet and watched the fairies till dawn.

Acknowledgements

For the cover, thanks must be divided evenly between Avery Dennis-Pavlich, brilliant designer; Levi Schroer, digital artist extraordinaire; David Israel, font wizard and generally pretty decent little brother; and rock_0407 of fiverr.com, who pulled it all together. Eternal gratitude goes to Enne Handley of Wild Hawk Editing for the sharp-eyed last-minute copyedit.

To my beta readers, some of whose names are "Mom," "Dad," "Grandma," and "Nana," but some of whom had no connection to me and thus no obligation whatsoever to open the document, and generously did so anyway—thank you for the love and the much-needed criticism. In particular, thank you to Ananya, real-life roommate, for reading my drafts, killing my spiders, and teaching me how to use the coffeemaker; and Nila, Italian fairy godmother, for laughing uproariously in the right places when I read my early efforts aloud.

On the other side of the pond, Rachel Nurse—Cardiffian born and bred—deserves accolades for dragging me out of my introvert cave and introducing me to such British institutions as breakfast at Spoons. The denizens of Aberdare Hall—most notably Fiona, Amarah, Elizabeth, and the Annas—have my thanks for adopting a certain jet-lagged American from day one.

And Dr. Juliette Wood probably doesn't remember me, because I spent the semester hiding in the back row of her lecture hall, but her class on Welsh mythology gave rise to this book.

Gillian—real-life curator of the Llangollen Museum, and probably not a fae guardian, though I couldn't swear to it—merits a paragraph of her own for taking in a starving student for a surreal long weekend in middle-of-nowhere Denbighshire. On the drive from the train station to her cottage, she pulled over at the edge of a sheep pasture and pointed to an anonymous bump in the grass. "That," she told me, "is an eleventh-century Norman motte," which pretty much set the tone for the next three days. She introduced me to Offa's Dyke and to Heather Dale's Arthurian album; she toted me along to a coffee meeting with an archaeologist and let me listen in; she taught me to pronounce the Welsh 'll'; and she introduced me to the ghosts of the hillfort across the street from her house. The most incredible afternoon of my semester was the one I spent sitting on a Stone Age rampart, listening to the wind whistle through the cairn at the heart of Moel Fenlli.

And to all the innocent passerby I waylaid for directions over my six months in your country—thank you, thank you, diolch yn fawr iawn!

www.ingramcontent.com/pod-product-compliance
Lightning Source LLC
Chambersburg PA
CBHW022200050726

47590CB00002B/598